THE WOLVES

A war in which men die in great numbers in mud-filled trenches is regarded with loathing. Yet often the same people justify the actions of small bands of men who fight behind enemy lines. These men are rarely depicted as vicious and brutal. Instead, they are considered daring, surmounting incredible odds and hardships: should one of them be fatally wounded, unselfishly he will stay behind to hold up the pursuing enemy ... In fact, the reality is somewhat different.

Books by Lawrence Williams
in the Linford Mystery Library:

THE MURDER TRIANGLE
IMAGES OF DEATH
A COPPER SNARE

LAWRENCE WILLIAMS

THE WOLVES

Complete and Unabridged

LINFORD
Leicester

First published in Great Britain

First Linford Edition
published 2006

British Library CIP Data

Williams, Lawrence, *1915* –
   The wolves.—Large print ed.—
Linford mystery library
   1. Detective and mystery stories
   2. Large type books
   I. Title
   823.9′14 [F]

ISBN 1–84617–570–4

Published by
F. A. Thorpe (Publishing)
Anstey, Leicestershire

Set by Words & Graphics Ltd.
Anstey, Leicestershire
Printed and bound in Great Britain by
T. J. International Ltd., Padstow, Cornwall

This book is printed on acid-free paper

With bitterness and contempt this book is dedicated to all who contributed to the success of the Manhattan Project

'All our best men are dead sir, and I'm not feeling too well myself.' And now the General laughed in such a high pitched and yet vigorous manner that Calvin was reminded of a young horse.
'For God's sake burn me Vicar . . . blow me up like a cartridge . . . set some powder under my bones and strew my pieces in the sea out there. Strew me like these damned mad flowers.'

The Flag: Robert Shaw

The lines from *The Flag*, by Robert Shaw, are quoted by kind permission of the author and of Chatto & Windus Ltd.

PART ONE

The Muster

1

Captain John Harding sighed as he put down the telephone. How like the C.O. to send for him now when there was so much to do. He stumped out of the office and got into his old car. He drove across the camp bad-temperedly clashing gears and wishing, for the thousandth time, he had never been transferred from his own work to a course in Biological and Gas Warfare. How the friends he had made in Gottingen would laugh if they knew what he was now doing.

All his protests had been overruled with the feeble excuse: 'Security prevents us putting you in the picture'. He had accepted this with his usual contempt for his so-called superior officers. Had he a little more humility he might have paused to query his own place 'in the picture'.

At the Admin. block he swung his car into a parking place, spattering other cars with gravel as he slewed to a halt. He stalked into the building, thumped on the Adjutant's door and walked in. He gave a perfunctory salute.

'Morning, Sir. The C.O. sent for me.'

'Good morning, John. He's expecting you.' Harding suddenly felt uneasy. The Adj. had not used his Christian name before; indeed, had never hidden his dislike for the supercilious young scientist from Oxford — the spoilt darling of the Research Unit.

'Something wrong, Sir?'

'You'll see. Go straight in.' The Adjutant looked shiftily in the direction of the inner office. Harding crossed the room and tapped gently on the door. It was immediately opened by the C.O.

'Come in, my boy. Come in.' He turned away from the door. 'Gentlemen, this is Captain Harding.'

There were two strangers sitting behind the C.O.'s desk. They were in civilian dress: dark suits, grey ties. They looked rather alike with grey hair, pale faces and the same air of weariness. They were not introduced to him by name. The C.O. shuffled his feet and coughed apologetically.

His awkwardness in dealing with Harding was more marked than usual.

'Sit down, Harding. These gentlemen have come to see you about a very serious matter.' Harding's habitually sulky expression became even more pronounced. Another dreary, time-wasting security check was about to start.

'Thank you, Colonel. We will explain.' It was the man on the right who spoke. The effect was extraordinary: the C.O. crept out of his own office. Harding was used to working with civilians but these two were obviously very special. The Old Man did not normally behave so meekly. Perhaps it was a serious matter after all. The man on the right spoke again.

'Harding, we want you for a special mission. You are the only person we can lay our hands on who fits the bill. Let me make that clear now and save ourselves a lot of useless argument.' He glanced across at the door through which the C.O. had vanished. Harding guessed there had already been one useless argument. 'We want a first-class physicist, working in your main field, who also knows something about gases, is known to be very fit and has had some battle experience. You are that man.'

There was a long pause but Harding refused to be drawn. He gazed steadily at the ornamental inkstand on the desk.

'As you know, German scientists are working on the same lines as us and we have evidence suggesting they are some way ahead. Of course that is no reflection on you.' There was another uncomfortable pause. 'They have set up a research centre in a remote part of Norway and we suspect they may be working either on methods of producing heavy water or researching into new gases. We want you to find out as much as you can about their research programme and then destroy the centre.

'You will be sent there with a small party which will be free to conduct the operation in any way which fits the situation. A Major Hurst will be in charge and you will retain your rank of Captain. The object of the exercise is to get you in the right place at the right time and the Major will act with this as his primary aim. He is very experienced and has just completed a not dissimilar operation in Italy. I'm sure this is an added incentive for you to volunteer. Your Commanding Officer assures us you will do so.'

The two strangers sat there patiently; the silence became oppressive. They were waiting for his enthusiastic answer — the eager young Captain jumping in to serve King and Country.

'How can I leave the course at this stage?'

'It's all arranged. You'll have a week to complete your studies and the Director will help you as much as he can. Then there'll be a week of preparation and you'll be posted from here in mid-June.'

'But I'm due to leave for the States later in the summer.'

'I regret to inform you that you have been rejected as unsuitable for the American project.'

'I've no choice have I?'

'No.' It was the man on the left speaking for the first time. He held out a folder. 'Take this into the Adjutant's office and read it carefully. Then bring it back here to me. It is a preliminary briefing with some unusual information included. This is an unusual operation.'

Harding stood up, took the file and put his hat on. He saluted: they gravely inclined their heads.

In the Adjutant's office the blinds were drawn and the C.O. was sitting with the back of his chair against the outer door. The Adjutant was fussing with a pile of papers. Without speaking, the C.O. pointed towards a chair in the corner. As Harding sat down he heard the clacking of boots on the polished floor as someone patrolled the corridor.

He worked his way through the file, dated May 1942. He was particularly impressed by two sections: one made it clear that the discovery of the research centre had been largely accidental; the other section summarised the preparations being made. Small groups of Commando and partisans were hiding stores and equipment in the mountains; each cache being placed close to but not in the valley in which the target was situated. As he read this he became depressed. He was being dragged into something gigantic and his was the crucial role. Worse still, he was becoming inextricably involved by the act of acquiring this information. 'Secrecy is best preserved by participation'. Where had he read that?

At the back of the file he found five sheets of notes stapled together. At the top of the first sheet was typed the headings: Comments on personnel selected for Operation Wolf. Underneath was a sub-heading: Officer Commanding: Major Alex Hurst. Then followed a summary of operations already carried out by the Major. Two passages had been underlined in green ink.

Relieved of his duties at a training centre after complaints of persistent brutality towards trainees. He was subsequently placed on active service (Special Operations) at his own request.

And further down the page:

This officer is nerveless. He claims to have killed sixty-eight of the enemy.

There is no reason to question this total.

The second sheet of paper dealt with the career of Sergeant Joe Reilly who suffered from the same blood lust as the Major. Harding shivered and turned the page.

The next two sheets of paper described the activities of Corporals Cooper and Jones who worked together. A list of their successful operations read like a travel brochure for Mediterranean Europe. Presumably they were always on operations. At the bottom of the second page was a note in green ink:

These two men have caused over one hundred deaths. A high proportion of these casualties was enemy service personnel.

Harding felt terribly sick. There was no doubt about the other casualties: civilians who got in the way. His chest tightened, he was choking, there was bile in the back of his mouth. He knew what he would find on the last sheet of paper: the record of 'Butcher Harding'. Those weary little men in the C.O.'s office had given plenty of thought to the arrangement of their file.

Poor bloody civilians who got in the way.

He was back in the rubble east of Dunkirk: Private Foster (real name Harding) who had joined the army without disclosing his name and academic record; without revealing the dreadful knowledge he had acquired. Private Harding moving east to meet Jerry moving west. Of its own volition his arm raised the paper before his eyes.

The enemy advanced on the position, sheltering behind a group of about fifty civilians. The advance was halted by the action of Private Harding who opened fire with an L.M.G. at very short range. The enemy suffered heavy casualties but several women and children were also killed. The position he was defending had to be abandoned thirty minutes after this incident.

11

The writer had not recorded everything: not the expression on the face of the child as his mother fell at his feet; not his cries as he fell across her body; not the way other soldiers refused to meet Harding's eyes. Their shame at not firing was as nothing measured against his guilt.

'Are you all right?' It was the C.O.

Harding looked at him but said nothing. Very carefully he put all the papers back into the file. He stood up. The C.O. spoke again but Harding did not hear him. He walked into the office where his visitors were waiting.

He *did* try to argue but it was a waste of breath. He was their man because of his abilities, skills and training, and also because they were prepared to use any device to put pressure on him. All three of them knew he had lost when they started arguing about the least important of his qualifications.

'We're not saying you're suitable because you shot some women and children, but because you've been under fire and when pressed you were prepared to shoot first and argue later.'

'But I didn't realise what I was doing. I didn't choose to shoot in a cold-blooded way. You can't blame me for an involuntary action in those circumstances.' He was nearly in tears.

'We're not blaming you. We're congratulating you.'

At that point he walked out of the office for the second time. He had no answers left in the face of such brutal reasoning and inflexibility of purpose.

A fortnight later he was ready to leave. His fellow scientists believed he was going to America and their envious good wishes had been the final irony. They even threw a party for him; very discreetly of course. The departure of a scientist for the U.S.A. could not be advertised in the Mess.

His last evening in the camp was a very quiet one. He was to be picked up at 23.30 hours, so after dinner he sat in his room and tried to read. As dusk fell the room became gloomy but he did not bother with the lights. He wanted a drink but could not face the social chatter and mild horse-play which junior officers were supposed to enjoy. Eventually, he lay down on his bed not expecting to sleep, but the strain of the last few days was catching up with him.

★   ★   ★

He was woken by his batman at 23.28.

'Your car is here, Sir,' he whispered, pulling down the blackout blinds.

Harding stood up, stretched nervously, switched on the lights.

'Thank you, Smith. Thank you for all your help while I've been here. Good luck with my old car.' There was an awkward pause. 'Time to say good-bye, Smith.'

'Good-bye, Sir, and thank you. I'm very pleased with the car. I hope I can fiddle some petrol somehow.'

Neither queried the fact they were whispering. Smith knew something odd was happening: 'A special do'. The Captain had sold him his car very cheaply, and now he was leaving without luggage, with empty pockets and with nothing to identify him. Smith did not know that details of his own posting had arrived that evening. He was to spend the rest of his war on an isolated, windswept camp in Scotland.

Harding walked silently down the corridor, his lanky, athletic figure moving cat-like over the worn carpet, through the side door and out into the night. A large, black car was waiting. The driver exchanged passwords with him and then locked him in the car. The blinds were down. Harding's irritation got the better of him and he flung up the blind over the glass partition separating him from the driver. Immediately, the driver's voice came crackling over a microphone.

'Sorry, Sir, the blinds must remain drawn.'

Harding shrugged his shoulders help-lessly. After the mistreatment he had suffered in the last few days pulling blinds in his face was a minor indignity. In the past week every item he possessed, private property as well as service issue, had been stripped from him. New, ill-fitting suits had been hung on him, altered and then whisked away. All he now owned were the new clothes he was wearing; even his watch was a replacement issue. He had signed innumerable undertakings of loyalty and good behaviour. Strangers had checked odd details of his background and taken him through reports about himself until he was dizzy. Obviously, many people had spent months checking on him before that fateful interview.

The longer he was questioned the more frightened he became. He was experienced enough to know how lax were British attitudes to security, yet he had been cross-questioned on every detail of his life. The only light relief had been provided by an earnest young psychologist who confessed he was puzzled by the fact Harding had joined the army. He pointed out that scientists came into war work as civilians but that he had chosen to join as a Private. Harding said he could not account for it either, unless he had done it in a fit of temper. This answer was very close to the truth but neither man realised it. The psychologist worked himself into a frenzy trying to invent some other reason which Harding found acceptable. Harding had enjoyed baiting him.

During this time no one mentioned any reasons for their investigations. He had asked questions but was answered with blank stares. When he realised why, he became even more frightened; his inquisitors were not feigning ignorance; none of them knew anything about the operation. He was the only person in the camp who knew the point of it all. Even the C.O. knew nothing of the operation itself.

Harding could not confide in anyone, could not ask advice, could not, as after Dunkirk, seek reassurances. The weight of this isolation was almost insupportable, but he was helped by the knowledge that he was already under test. Nevertheless, by the end of the period he was becoming mentally exhausted; so exhausted that his chaffeur need not have worried about the blinds. Harding slept as if he were dead while his body was carried secretly through the English countryside.

2

He woke with a sore head and a mouthful of gravel. The car had stopped. The driver told him to raise the blinds, and when he did so the soft light of early morning splashed into his face. The windows darkened again as two M.P.s stepped up to the car, stared at him and compared him with photographs they carried. The insolence of this scrutiny enraged him; it confirmed the frightful idea that his rank might not count any more. He scowled back at them. Then, to complete his loss of face, he heard them discussing him with the driver. What did they mean by asking if he had given any trouble? He heard the driver laugh, then one of the guards said: 'Right, Bill! Take him away!'

They drove on for about a mile and then turned off the narrow lane into a long, dark drive bordered by high rhododendrons. Two hundred yards from the lane they were halted at another check point. The driver gave a password, the gate was opened and they drove through. At last they drew up before the house.

It was a magnificent Georgian mansion set in sweeping lawns shaded by tall cedars which spread black against the dawn sky. The light was not yet good enough to see what lay beyond the lawns but one could guess at rose gardens, an orchard and a lake. The driver unlocked the door and Harding climbed unsteadily from the car to stand spellbound before the white house as the dawn caught the east windows and set them flaming.

The spell was broken by the slamming of the car door. He turned to speak to his driver but the car was already rolling forward. He half-raised his hand but the driver ignored him. As the car disappeared from view he stood forlornly before the great house. He felt strangely disoriented. It was the feeling he had known when his parents' divorce came through; he was once more a pawn in the hands of people who knew so much more than he did. Before he could wallow in self-pity a short, plump, elderly lady came out of the great white house and down the steps to meet him.

'Good morning, Captain Harding.' They shook hands formally. 'Welcome to my house. You are the second member of your party to arrive; Major Hurst is already here. Please come with me and I'll show you to your room.' As he followed her up the steps he caught sight of someone watching them from a first floor window. Then the curtain swung back into position.

He was led across a spacious entrance hall, up a magnificent staircase and along a carpeted corridor on the first floor. Vases of flowers stood at every corner, pictures crowded the walls. A soothing atmosphere of quiet luxury enfolded him. His smiling guide gave him a key and left him to unlock his own door. As he thanked her he wondered how often she had met miserable guests and cheered them with the warmth of her smile and the charm of her home.

His room was very large, newly decorated and luxuriously furnished. A door on the far side of the room led into his own private bathroom. Feeling considerably happier he walked to the window. His room was at the back of the house and he had a superb view across lawns and lake towards distant mist-brushed hills rising up into the strengthening light of early morning. In the branches of a tree some twenty yards from his window a blackbird began to sing. It was the perfect opening to a summer day. The contrast with the ugly affairs of men suddenly overwhelmed him. He turned from the view and flung himself face down on the bed.

Later, he made a closer inspection of his room and discovered that the wardrobe bulged with suits, and that the chest of drawers was equally well-stocked. Everything he might want had been supplied. He was again impressed by the efficiency of his masters; it was only a week ago he had been measured for the suit he was wearing.

After a hot bath, which eased some of the tension out of him and reduced the size of the gravel in his mouth, he put on some of his new clothes and then went back to his window. As he leaned out to enjoy the view the smell of frying bacon wafted up to him.

His reverie was interrupted by a knock on the door. He opened it and hastily stepped back. He was facing the biggest man he had ever seen.

'I'm Major Hurst.'

'How do you do, Sir. I'm Harding.'

'Prove it.'

As they went through the sequence of passwords Harding gaped up at him. He was built like a tank: a square, powerful figure with enormous shoulders. He stood with his head pushed forward and chin jutting out. His coarse, florid complexion was almost negroid. But it was the eyes that were most impressive: hard, brilliant grey eyes that stared through Harding as he mumbled the idiotic phrases of identification. He felt his own gaze crumbling away before the intensity of this inspection. He blinked nervously.

'So you're Harding, the brilliant young scientist I've got to wet-nurse. Well, well!' He stood silent for a moment. Then: 'Tell me, Harding, do you know what this is all about?'

'I've only seen a brief summary of the situation, Sir.'

'Just a brief summary, eh?' He laughed unpleasantly. 'Bet they wouldn't show you any more in case you funked it.'

'It does happen to be top secret, Sir.' He was already loathing the man.

'Well, I've picked a bloody good team to look after you. If we can't protect you no one can.'

'Thank you.' He knew he need not conceal his dislike. Hurst obviously enjoyed hostility.

'We might as well go down to breakfast now. I know Cooper and Jones will be there to meet us. They've just arrived. I saw them from my window.'

Harding locked his door and they walked along the corridor together. At the top of the stairs Hurst turned to him and said, 'By the way, only you and I have seen the summaries of our service careers, so no one else in the party knows our respective pasts, at least, not in that sort of detail.' He gave what was intended to be a conspiratorial smile. It came out as a sinister leer.

The dining-room was almost full. A pretty waitress showed them to a table set for five. Two men sitting there stood up as they arrived and Hurst introduced them to Harding. Corporal Andrew Cooper was a short, dark, secretive man. Corporal Harry Jones was a tall, sneering blond. The only thing they obviously had in common was a strong cockney accent; not that either of them had much to say once introductions were completed. They gave their full attention to the excellent breakfast, and as Hurst took his cue from them Harding was free to look round at the other guests.

There were about thirty men and women in the room, mostly men, sitting in groups varying from two to six in number. None of them talked much but they all ate heartily. The few remarks that were made were in strongly accented English. Harding assumed they were all involved in special operations of some sort and wondered how many of them were soon to return to their own countries, and if some, like him, were training for their first job.

His attention was especially drawn to a lovely blonde girl in a pale blue dress. Could she be mixed up in that sort of thing? Was she an experienced agent or a beginner like himself? The latter, surely?

After breakfast, Hurst suggested they go to his room. As they left the dining room their hostess appeared, gave Hurst an envelope and told him to read the contents carefully. He looked slightly puzzled but asked no questions. At that moment an aircraft passed low over the house. 'That'll be Reilly, right on time. Please send him straight up to my room, Ma'am.'

In the Major's room they sat in arm-chairs and waited for Reilly. Hurst read through the notes he had been given. Jones and Cooper dozed. Harding spent the time wondering if Reilly would be as unprepossessing as the rest of his companions. Perhaps he was being unfair; they were neatly dressed and appeared to be waiting for the start of a board meeting. Then he looked into their faces;

faces composed of angular planes, deep tense lines; faces harsh and closed even when relaxed; faces of men from another world; a world of horrors and terrors he had never known. He had to enter that world.

There was a knock on the door. Cooper and Jones were instantly awake, Hurst looked up from his papers and Reilly burst in on them. Short, stocky, dark and unshaven, he greeted them brusquely.

'Morning, Major. Morning you two: Cooper and Jones I presume.' Then he paused and stared at Harding. Hurst introduced them. 'So, you're the new boy are you? Well sonny, welcome to the nastiest collection of rogues I know. The scum of the British Army. But don't worry. I'm here to look after you and so is my lucky mascot.'

'What's that?' asked Hurst.

'Why, Nina. You must have seen her. The blonde bit downstairs. Dutch, very charming. Met her once before and the job I was on turned out a hundred per cent successful. She'll see we're all right.'

'You keep off,' said Hurst, grinning

affectionately at the Sergeant. 'Top brass don't like agents getting pregnant. Never mind this old ram, lads. He's not what I'd call a good example to follow. Well then, let's make a start by going down to the garden.' They looked at him in surprise but no one questioned the order.

In the garden they sat in the centre of the lawn. It was not lost on three of them that Hurst chose a spot away from the terrace and away from the trees. Harding was more concerned about the dew-drenched lawn spoiling his suit.

'I've brought you out here because of what's in this envelope,' said Hurst. 'The papers include a note which makes it clear our security will be tested in the next few hours. We can't afford to be caught out so I thought we would avoid any worries about being overheard. The security officers at this centre identify themselves with one of these.' He passed round a small, red identity card. 'They don't wear uniform and they change both staff and cards quite frequently. Of course, we'll be informed about card changes but keep your wits about you;

anyone here could be a security man — or woman.'

'Well, we're going to be here for some time so we must accept their methods. Talk to anyone you like but make no attempt to discuss their work or yours. That goes for Joe's pretty friend as well. You can write letters but give them to our hostess unsealed. She will fill in an address which has nothing to do with this place. Do not try to find out where we are and do not leave the house and grounds. Everything we could possibly need for this operation will be brought to us; I have only to ask our hostess. By the way, she is senior to me so we all address her as Ma'am.'

'Are we not to know her name?' Harding asked the question involuntarily.

There was a long silence. He wished he could burrow into the flawless lawn. The others stared at his red face.

'Oh dear,' said Reilly, giving a perfect imitation of Harding's Oxford accent. 'Oh dear me. Wake up sonny, for Christ's sake! The more you know the more you can tell. Didn't they teach you that at

College? This place is a very special centre so we don't want to know too much about it, do we?' Harding swallowed his rage, shook his head. Reilly shrugged his shoulders and looked appealingly at Hurst who grinned but said nothing. Cooper gave a snort of disgust, while Jones sneered at the daisy he had just decapitated.

'You'll learn,' said Hurst, at last. 'Just remember that anyone you speak to may be out to trip you and then you'll be spared any further embarrassment. You've got to take this security business seriously you know. If we don't keep our wits about us we may jeopardise our lives while we are here as effectively as if we make a mistake behind enemy lines.

'Well, I'm now going to give you a preliminary briefing. You will not be briefed further for at least a month. Yes, a month! We are going to be here a long time preparing for this job. I know some of us are already in operational trim, as it were, but this job is so big, so vital we are going to turn ourselves into a perfect fighting unit. No punches will be pulled and I intend to be absolutely frank with you when discussing your progress.

'Now, when you've done other jobs you've been told how important they were: you would win the war in a week etc. This time what I am going to say is absolutely true.' He paused, then, 'We are going to get some information from Jerry that can shorten the war. If we fail we may lose the war. It's as tight as that.'

They absorbed this in silence, impressed and depressed by his simple statement.

'To be precise, it is Captain Harding who will get this information, the rest of us are merely bodyguards on this job. I was told to get the best so I picked you. You two, Cooper and Jones, don't have to prove anything to Reilly and myself. I know you're bloody good so let's not waste time playing team games among ourselves. I'm in charge and I'll assume you are good enough to cope with any orders I give. The quicker we become one team the longer we'll live.'

Cooper looked thoughtfully at Jones and then nodded. 'O.K. by us, Major.'

'Harding is a scientist working in the

field of — of explosives. Jerry has scientists working in the same field; at least, we think it's the same field. We know where they are working and could stop them quite easily, but that is not the main aim. We have to find out how far they've got, how far their ideas might help us and then, and only then, destroy the plant. Harding's been chosen to come with us, not only because he is a scientist, but also because he had some battle experience at Dunkirk and is also very fit. If the war had not started he would have run the Marathon at the 1940 Olympics.'

If Hurst hoped to increase confidence in Harding by these revelations he misjudged his audience completely. Cooper burst out laughing and said: 'He'll be wiv us when we're running away, then.' The others chuckled spitefully. Hurst said nothing, leaving Harding to wonder if the Major was really trying to help him get established in the group. Then Hurst held up his hand for silence; playing the part of the benevolent chairman entertaining his fellow directors.

'I can't give you full details of the target

at this stage. What I can tell you is that we'll be working in tough country. We have to wear foreign clothing and use German weapons. We must not be taken alive and our wounded must walk. If anyone is killed in action nothing on him will betray his nationality. Just as we have arrived here without personal possessions so will we arrive in enemy territory. Some of you are used to this set-up but I promise you things will be tighter and tougher than you've ever known before.

'We have full backing from the few people who know about us. We can ask for anything we want except alterations to the time schedule; that is absolutely fixed by weather conditions and time of year. As far as equipment is concerned you may suggest alterations at any time, but you may not use British materials.

'Lastly, to emphasise the importance of this job I must tell you that supply dumps for us are already being set up by Commando and partisan units. This is being done in such a way that no suspicion of our interest in the area is aroused. Well, any questions?'

In the silence Harding recollected how he had felt when this information had first been given to him. Then Reilly spoke.

'I suppose this operation is in Norway. Will we be given any climbing instruction?'

'How did you work that out?' asked Hurst.

'I know you, you old fox. You said 'partisans' so it isn't Germany. Then you talked about time of year and season. We were both in Norway in 1940 and we both speak Norwegian. Don't forget we've worked together before.'

'You've guessed right. I wasn't supposed to tell you that yet, but I don't suppose it will matter very much. As far as climbing is concerned I don't anticipate anything tougher than hill walking. I think if we get really fit and can move as a team we'll cope with any difficulties we meet.'

'You know more than you're telling,' said Reilly.

Hurst grinned at him but did not reply. There was another long pause.

'No more questions? Very well. We start by checking equipment. Follow me!'

They scrambled to their feet and followed Hurst across the lawn. Harding thought his companions now resembled gangsters as they slouched ahead of him. The incongruousness of their clothes and of the setting, when related to the task facing them, heightened the air of tension and expectancy which surrounded these men. The brutal directness of Hurst's short briefing had increased this tension. Harding was faced with new, strange attitudes to which he had quickly to adjust; a process made doubly difficult by the fact that his companions did not find such attitudes at all strange.

Hurst led them round the side of the house to the stable yard. The stables were arranged round three sides of the courtyard with the fourth side open to the drive that led past the house and down to the lake. The courtyard was deserted except for an old man who was sitting on the ground with his back against a wall and dozing in the sun. Beside him was a broom; an excuse for his presence there. Hurst marched across to one of the stables and unlocked the door. As he did so he looked across at the sleeping figure and grinned savagely. He kicked open the door and they trooped into the cool shade. Hurst snapped down a light switch to reveal a dusty, unkempt storehouse of packing cases and old straw.

'Check it!' ordered Hurst. Harding's companions immediately spread out, kicking aside piles of straw, moving cases, tapping beams and generally behaving like ferrets; or so it seemed to Harding. Yet he was aware he had missed something; they were a jump ahead of him again. (This feeling was soon to become permanent.) Not knowing quite what to do he walked round the stable and counted the cases. He was embarrassed by his companions' earnestness.

'All clear?' asked Hurst. A variety of grunts and muttered imprecations confirmed that all was clear. Harding was biting on his tongue to check a facetious remark when he realised Hurst was glaring at him. 'All clear, Harding?'

'Nineteen packing cases, Sir.' What made him give such a stupid answer he did not know, but some guardian angel must have been busy.

'Ah,' sighed Hurst. 'You've got it.' Then turning on the other three, 'Open these cases as quick as you can. Only eighteen were delivered yesterday.'

The fifth case they broke open contained a tape recorder. They watched it slowly revolving, ensnaring every sound they made. The Major bent down, switched it off and then played it back.

They heard first the muffled sound of footsteps and the loud banging of a hammer as the case was nailed down. Then, eerie and frightening, the grinding sound of the stable door being locked. At this point Hurst's face became a rich magenta colour but he managed to control his temper. The tape was silent for about two minutes, then they heard their own arrival faithfully reproduced. Every sound had been captured: Hurst's orders, Cooper's laugh, a curse from Jones as he banged against a case, muttered imprecations from Reilly and, cutting through all these, a solemn, youthful voice chanting: 'One, two, three . . . ' Harding felt the blush on his cheeks. Then Hurst switched off.

They stared at each other; that two minutes silence was worrying. 'Get him!' growled Hurst.

Jones and Cooper dived through the doorway. Within seconds the sleepy old man was standing in front of them with Cooper and Jones gripping his arms. He grinned cheerfully at his captors. 'You soon found it, I must say.'

'Never mind,' snarled Hurst. 'There should only be one key. Where is the other one?'

'Your excellent hostess has it. She has duplicate keys for every door in the place. She let me in and locked up when I'd finished. You only just missed her. As for me, well you know all about me from the notes she gave you at breakfast.'

Hurst stared at him for a long time. Then: 'Let him go. Take your bloody recorder with you. The only good thing about this is that now we know you they can't use you any more.'

The cleaner grinned triumphantly and walked over to the packing case. As he did so Hurst signalled to Reilly. The old man was allowed to get as far as the door, then Reilly stepped in front of him. Hurst leered down at their unwelcome visitor who now turned rather pale. His confidence evaporated; he was in the wrong place with the wrong people. The possibility that he might never get out had not previously occurred to him.

'Just a minute, Pop,' said Hurst. 'How about a little identification?' The old man sighed and put down the tape recorder.

'Here you are.' He produced a red card identical to the one they had looked at a short time before. 'I can see we need not worry too much about *your* security.'

'Now the tape,' said Hurst.

'What do you mean?'

'You know exactly what I mean. You fail on every count and you're nearly dead.'

Harding shivered as he watched Hurst rip the tape from the recorder. It was not so much the security game that affected him as the cold ferocity of his companions.

'Now get out!' snapped Hurst, pushing the recorder into the old man's chest.

Shakily, he sidled between Hurst and Reilly and scuttled away across the yard. They never saw him again. Gloomily, Harding watched him go. Like the old man he had not regarded security as a matter of life and death for himself; but the rest of the group had learnt through bitter experience that it was so. Two different worlds had just collided and the clash drove home the imminence of the dangers they were to share.

'Well, now you know,' said Hurst. 'They'll try anything to keep us on our toes.'

'We should've wrung his bleedin' neck,' growled Jones.

'Don't worry, there'll be other opportunities,' said Hurst. 'Get into denims and we'll start real work.'

They took three days to unpack and check every item. The arsenal which they discovered delighted Harding's companions. When they had finished cleaning and checking everything the stable looked like a private museum of war. There were rubber dinghies, life jackets, flares, medical kits, iron rations, German uniforms, Norwegian anoraks, ropes, capes, groundsheets, boots, and weapons of every kind. Harding had never before seen so many German small arms and so much ammunition collected together; he estimated they each had a choice of eight guns. His companions did not appear to regard this as excessive so he kept his mouth shut.

3

On the fourth day they began their training programme. Dressed in denims, festooned with weapons, they clambered into a small truck and were driven by Reilly through the grounds to a rifle range.

They spent the whole day on 'familiarisation', as Hurst described it. They began with two hours of test firing; ten rounds at every hundred yards from one hundred to eight hundred yards. Then they returned to the one hundred mark and fired kneeling, then prone, on the run, from the shoulder, and from the hip, according to rapid orders from Hurst.

They rested between exercises but by mid-afternoon Harding was so tired and confused he was no longer fully aware of what he was doing. His misery was increased by the fact that his companions were improving their performances all the time. They responded just as quickly to commands as they had in the morning, and they were hitting their targets with greater accuracy.

Firing ended at five o'clock but there was no rest for them. As soon as they got back to the stables every weapon was stripped down, every part was examined and cleaned. There was a short break for dinner and then they went back to work. As weapons were replaced in the racks Harding noticed that some of them had small scratches and pieces of sticky tape on their stocks. Hurst explained that they were marking weapons for their own reference, grading them according to performance. Harding realised that if this was so and the others were already selecting weapons he would be left with what they didn't want. But that night he was too tired to care. He could almost feel Hurst's disapproval at his lack of enthusiasm but he pretended he was unaware of it.

When the last gun had been reassembled and the tool kits put away they all went to Hurst's room. He spoke to them quietly, analysing faults in each man's work and commenting on some of the guns they had used. He was completely frank and spared no one, but he dropped his hectoring manner completely. Harding was so struck by this change he wondered if Hurst knew that bullying did not lead to improvements; perhaps the Major was a much deeper character than he had suspected. Harding was unaware there was any element of superiority in his thinking.

As soon as debriefing was completed and orders given for the next day, Harding left the others, went to his room, bathed and fell into bed. He slept solidly until breakfast.

The second day at the range was devoted entirely to tests of accuracy. The tests highlighted Harding's ineptness and Hurst bawled him out in front of the others. He had to stand there and take it; protests about rank and protocol were a waste of breath in a group only interested in performance. Then Hurst slipped back into his role of fatherly adviser, took Harding to one side and gave him some helpful tips. Later in the day it was

Cooper's turn to err and Hurst gave him the full treatment. It was another virtuoso performance and it left Cooper dusky red and shaking with fury. Harding felt sorry for him but Jones and Reilly were helpless with mirth. Reilly, the only one to have worked with Hurst before, kept thumping Jones in the ribs with his elbow and whispering, 'Told you he was bloody good, didn't I? You don't often hear language like this. Listen to 'im going it!'

In the afternoon Hurst started them on a new set of exercises. They went to the indoor range and practised with pistols for the first time. Harding had never fired a Mauser before and at first found it difficult to control, but once he had mastered it he showed his best form. For the first time he returned scores as good as anyone else and Hurst was quick to congratulate him. By the time they returned to the rifle range he was feeling very pleased with himself. Fifty rounds at six hundred yards soon put him back in his place; he was competing with the best shots in the British Army.

The third and last day of the series was

devoted to a mixture of exercises using all the weapons in their stores. At the debriefing Hurst was complimentary about all their performances and suggested they should each select their personal arms from the stock they had been using. This took some time and led to some arguments, but at last the weapons were rearranged in their racks in six groups — one group for each of them and a large set of spares.

'I must order some more ammunition now,' said Hurst, smiling. 'I understand the boys at the range will be glad to see the back of us; they reckon it takes them the whole evening to clear away the mounds of cases we leave behind. However, they haven't seen the last of us by any means. Although we have to start sharing the ranges with other groups we'll still be firing every morning. In the afternoons I think we'll turn our attention to getting fit.'

They all looked down their noses at this except Harding who felt excited by the prospect. He knew he was fit and could show his colleagues there was one sphere in which he was ahead of them. He still had a lot to learn.

The next afternoon was a disaster. They spent half an hour in the gym with a P.T. instructor who led them through a varied programme of simple exercises. This gentle warm-up gave no hint of what was to follow. Even when they piled into their little truck to go to the assault course Harding wasn't particularly worried. However, his confidence began to sag when they arrived. The course was laid out in a secluded part of the grounds and consisted of a fearsome set of closely spaced obstacles, each demanding techniques quite outside the experience of a marathon runner.

They went round the course together at a slow pace, taking each obstacle carefully. They arrived back at the start covered in mud and perspiration. Hurst smiled gently and suggested that perhaps they should now make a race of it.

Reilly gave him an odd look but said nothing. Rather self-consciously they arranged themselves in a ragged line and then Hurst shouted, 'Go!'

Harding rushed at the first obstacle, a twelve feet high timber wall, hoping to get clear of the others; he thought he would be slower on the obstacles but faster on the ground. He leapt at the wall, caught the top beam and pulled himself up. As he rolled over and dropped to the ground Reilly collided with him and they fell awkwardly. Harding recovered and raced on, slightly ahead of everyone else.

The next hazard was a deep ditch, twenty-five feet across; the only way to cope with it was to jump as far as possible and scramble up the far side. As Harding took off Reilly bumped him again, he lost his balance and crashed to the bottom of the pit. By the time he had climbed out he was last in the field and Reilly was at the next obstacle. This consisted of a horizontal beam, about eighteen feet from the ground and draped with nets on both sides; these were not fixed to the ground so that as they were climbed they swayed violently from side to side.

Harding began climbing as the others came down. Halfway up he came face to face with Reilly descending the other net.

For a moment they hung there separated only by the netting. Reilly grinned happily, then Harding fell to the ground and rolled over, clutching his stomach where the Sergeant's knee had caught him.

He covered the next part of the course in a daze of pain and rage. He was now far behind and knew he would soon suffer the humiliation of meeting the others coming back.

He met them at the 'water jump': a broad pond about twenty yards across. Above it a beam stood on supports and extended halfway across the pond. At the end of this shaky pier two ropes led on to the other bank: one rope to walk on and one to hang on. Thus the crossing was completed rather like a tram with one rail and an overhead cable. As Harding arrived, Hurst, Jones and Cooper were just completing the return crossing. He stood aside to let them pass. He scarcely heard their ribald comments. He was watching Reilly.

As the Sergeant started back towards the middle of the pond, using the ropes,

Harding cat-walked along the beam to meet him. The other three, aware of the tension, had stopped to watch. Harding reached the end of the beam, stretched up and jerked the upper rope as hard as he could. Reilly turned a somersault and disappeared in a cloud of spray.

Harding's triumph was short-lived. As Reilly surfaced at the end of the beam he jerked Harding's legs away from under him and dragged him into the water. The next few seconds were a chaotic jumble of panicky splashing, shouting, threshing arms and legs and misdirected blows. Reilly and Harding were dragged from the pond and dumped on the bank. Cooper and Jones, helpless with laughter, stood between them.

Harding sat in the mud, head in hands, wishing he were dead. Dimly, he heard someone congratulating him on his survival. Then the roaring in his ears took coherent form: it was Hurst bawling at Reilly who was grinning broadly. Then, to make the message absolutely clear, Hurst led the other three off at a gallop and left Harding on the ground.

He trailed miserably after them, finding no consolation in the suspicion that the whole thing was a put-up job.

This incident marked the start of what Cooper aptly named 'The Ten Day Terror'. From that day on Hurst drove them unmercifully: the range in the mornings, unarmed combat and P.T. in the afternoons and, as a last refinement, evening classes to improve their German. He never missed an opportunity to extend them, insult them, or set them at each other's throats. He broke down any semblance of team spirit and reduced them to four quarrelsome individuals. Only once was any protest made: Jones objected to covering the assault course carrying a full pack. As a result they did it twice.

Only once were the five of them united in their anger: when they heard that Tobruk had fallen.

The extreme toughness of their programme reflected the toughness of the problems facing Hurst. The biggest of these was how to integrate, on an operational basis, the inexperienced Captain with a group of four men already fully aware of their own enormous capabilities. He had to keep them working on a variety of demanding exercises without killing Harding in the process.

One solution he adopted was to alternate short periods of extreme stress with less demanding exercises which Harding could manage quite well. Secondly, he placed great emphasis on team training and team achievements rather than on individual skill; thus success or failure befell two or more members of the group in each exercise. This gave some protection to Harding who sometimes achieved the highest standards by intelligently combining his own efforts with the more experienced efforts of one or two of his companions.

This approach helped with another problem since it prevented Cooper and Jones always working together. They had to operate just as efficiently with other team members as with each other. Cooper and Jones accepted these arrangements because they knew the team would function best on this basis. As for Reilly, he never had disputed Hurst's authority and, being closest to him, he found the training easier to bear than did Cooper and Jones.

Harding was in no fit state to dispute anything. His physical exhaustion and mental confusion were such that he was incapable of making any protest against the brutality inflicted on them. He knew Hurst had to drive home the fundamental point that they all had weaknesses as well as strengths; that they had to recognise what each of them had to offer to the others when under pressure. Knowing this did not make life any more bearable.

Dunkirk had given Harding the essential touch of fear that every green soldier needs before he can be really effective; but that had happened a long time ago, had been a brief experience and had not been repeated. It had also taken place while he was an ordinary soldier sharing in the state of raw inexperience and criminal unpreparedness that characterised so much of the British Army at that time. That past experience bore no relation to his present situation.

There were harder things to accept. He had to acknowledge, by his co-operation and determination to learn, that he was something of a passenger; a parasite who expected to be sustained by other people's blood and courage. The whole operation depended on his willingness to accept the humiliation this would entail. His brilliance of mind, fitness of body, his tragic gleaning of battle experience entitled him to nothing. He was merely a recording device which had to be set up, switched on and off, and then dragged back to England. The fact he also had to shoot as straight and march as far as his companions was just his hard luck as far as they were concerned.

The rigidity with which his companions clung to this view was made more severe by their rejection of him as a friend. The longer they worked together the clearer it became that acquaintanceship was not going to develop into friendship. He had to accept that the only type of friendship possible was of the kind shared by Reilly and Hurst: friendship that was forged in shared battle experience and had nothing to do with the casual comradeship of a training course. At first, he was bitterly resentful of this rejection and of his own loneliness. Later, it occurred to him that his colleagues might be the only survivors of their original teams because they had worried least about their team mates as friends. He felt obscurely ashamed of himself as he thought of this; ashamed of his stupidity rather than his attempt to romanticise his unprepossessing companions.

The realities of the schism between himself and the others he was not yet prepared to examine. The real truth was that none of his companions were ever going to like him much; any more than he was going to like them. For Jones he had complete contempt; the man was no better than a wild animal for whom even Cooper's regard was suspect. For the rest, he could not hide his disgust at their attitudes and their disregard for what he privately thought of as the fundamental decencies of life.

It was some time before Harding accepted that the factor arousing their contempt for him was his hypocrisy in regarding them as callous and brutal when he was helping to develop new and more horrible forms of destruction. When he eventually realised this fact he loathed them even more.

The physical strain of 'The Ten Day Terror' was also very great. Harding found his life controlled by awareness of aching feet, of blisters, of underclothing so shrunken with his own sweat that every seam chaffed his skin. An infinite number of small bruises gradually coalesced over the whole of his strained, maltreated body. Worst of all was the ache of exhaustion experienced as burning grit in his eyes, as a continuous pain in the top of his head, as a desperate, agonising longing for sleep. He felt that only sleep could save him. But sleep they were denied; night exercises had become part of their training.

Hurst was fully aware of the stresses within the group and within each individual, but he believed that discipline was a more valuable link between guerrilla fighters than friendship. He knew from experience that bravery, determination and concern for each other were not enough. He had seen more than one group of brave men cut to pieces because of a lack of fundamental discipline. He knew that all his team were used to working outside the normal service environment, and he had wondered if he might have to make the point about discipline very forcefully. To his relief no one ever questioned his aim for perfect discipline. The atmosphere in which they worked, the tensions generated in the group, pointed the obvious lessons. A faulty safety catch or an untied bootlace might betray them; hesitation in carrying out an order would mean disaster.

They also accepted the fact that different members of the team would be in charge in different circumstances. No one questioned Harding's orders when dealing with identification and destruction of scientific apparatus. No one questioned Reilly's authority when they were training with different types of German firearms. At the same time, Hurst's willingness to draw on the expertise of team members did not deceive anyone into thinking he was loosening the tight reins of command.

As they became more deeply involved in their work, as they became more dependent on each other's special skills, their personal differences were buried. Hurst had made them indispensable to each other. His qualities as a commander had seen to that. His forceful personality was such that even when he insisted on repeating a simple, familiar task many times they believed he did so because it mattered. His own enormous toughness and legendary reputation stood him in good stead, even in that rugged company, and he did not have to waste time and energy proving his fitness to command. In this he was helped by Reilly who was forever bombarding his companions with fantastic tales from the past he had shared with Hurst. As Cooper put it rather waspishly one evening, 'If ten per cent of wot you tell us is true then the Major's the bloke for the job.'

4

At the end of their third week together Hurst began to slacken the pressure. So well judged was his timing, so well had he assessed them, that they responded without recriminations. They were becoming a team because they had been forced to accept each other as fellow sufferers under intense pressure. They had become united in a mutual licking of wounds.

Hurst was now confident that they would operate as a team while in the field; it was unlikely they would be subjected to similar pressures for so great a length of time while on the operation. Other pressures, which could not be simulated by any form of training, would have to be faced if and when they arose. Hurst could only hope that Harding would accept the realities of war as well as he was now accepting the demands of training with four professional killers.

One evening, Hurst suggested they

meet for drinks in his room to celebrate the completion of a month together. They were taken aback, not at the idea of drinking in his room, but by the realisation they had been together a month. In spite of all their grim work, or perhaps because of it, time had slipped away almost unnoticed. Only in the dining-room had time registered: the disappearance of familiar faces, the arrival of new groups, marked the irregular but persistent pulse of war. As for drinking in the Major's room — this was normal procedure now he had relaxed a little. They told each other it helped security to drink there instead of in the bar, but they all knew the real reason. The bar, like the dining room, was full of ghosts. One could not help thinking of those who had disappeared. That lovely Dutch girl, so calm and self-possessed: was she still free or in the hands of the Gestapo? What of others they had known? The least sensitive of them found the bar oppressive; a funeral parlour run by undertakers in carnival mood.

When they had made themselves

comfortable in the armchairs, bottles within reach, and when Reilly had checked the room for any sign of eavesdroppers, Hurst gave his usual talk on the day's work. When he had finished he hesitated before starting his briefing for the next day. They watched him. He drained his glass and stared into it for a moment.

'Well,' he said, he always began with the same word, 'I promised you at least a month of preparation and we finished it today. I'm sure you want to know what happens next.' Another long pause, the air brittle with tension, then: 'We go some time next month.'

Their chairs were no longer comfortable. They eyed each other nervously, made fatuous gestures: raised eyebrows, shrugged shoulders. Hurst coughed harshly and they resettled themselves.

'We have to go in August because conditions are likely to be at their best then. Our target is in a latitude where there is about six hours darkness every night in mid-August, and, at that time, the weather will not have become so grim that we'll not survive on the high plateau country of the fjeld. We will also have a choice of unsettled weather with some nights cloudy, some nights clear. This will give us a choice of days for arrival and departure and will permit a little flexibility in deciding when to hit the target. It may also allay the fears of the enemy if one or two black nights pass without incident.'

'Are they expecting us?' asked Cooper.

'Not as far as we know. Our friends operating in the area have been very discreet and Jerry hasn't done anything unexpected in the last few weeks. I doubt if we have anything to worry about from that point of view. I was thinking more on the lines that we might have to lie low if we accidently bump Jerry on our way to the target. Then it would be helpful if several good nights pass without us making a move.

'Of course, there is one vital reason why we must go this summer: our top scientists are worried stiff that Jerry may be some way ahead of us in their research. If this is so we dare not delay. In any case our backroom boys are so worried it will be a valuable service just to relieve their anxieties — if we can.

'Well, starting tomorrow, we go to the range every other morning. The remaining mornings will start in the gym and then we'll attend briefings on the target. Every afternoon we'll be coached in the uses of various pieces of Jerry equipment including a new and powerful type of two-way radio. It will be our link for reporting results of the operation and arranging details of our return.

'From now on I can only outline the programme for you, partly because we will be in the hands of instructors we haven't yet met and also because neither I nor Harding know the precise location of the target or the date of departure. All this vital stuff will come up in the briefings next week. I doubt if we will be held back much beyond the middle of the month, but I'm not absolutely certain about that.

'Lastly, I must remind you, even if it insults you, that security is vital. Every day now we are going to learn more about this operation so that we'll become bigger risks every day. You can expect the security boys on the site to close in on us again as from now. From midnight tonight, identification is by this green card. The red card is now obsolete.' He passed round the sample card for them to read. Then he poured himself another beer. 'Well, drink up lads. I think we need an early night.'

They drank up almost absent-mindedly and then wandered back to their own rooms. All five of them had some difficulty getting to sleep.

⋆ ⋆ ⋆

The next morning there was a security check. They had to stay in their rooms and watch security staff go through their kit looking for anything that might betray a detail of the operation. At last: 'Your boys are clean, Major.' Sighs of relief but no slackening of tension.

'Bet the Major arranged that check,' growled Reilly, as he and Harding walked down the corridor together. Harding raised his eyebrows but Reilly nodded vigorously. 'It's all part of getting us keyed up. I've worked with this boyo before and this is true to form.' They were keyed up all right, even those who were used to living on a razor's edge.

The days now tumbled over them in a flood of exercises and briefings. Contact with the outside world dwindled away; isolation was now desired. Even Reilly's demands for a woman, once a constant source of amusement and irritation, had now ceased. No one wanted to write letters. No one listened to the radio any more; someone else could tell them if the war was over and they didn't have to go. They had successfully constructed a savage world of their own into which they all fitted; any external contacts were intolerable distractions. Even their instructors were now treated with a curtness that gave offence; as soon as a class or briefing finished the group turned in on itself, shutting out the outsiders. A fortnight earlier they might have stood their instructors a drink before dinner, but not now.

Hurst presided over this little world like a benevolent she-wolf. He treated them with a fierce, possessive tenderness which only exploded into wrath when someone bungled a command. Quietly and effectively he braced them for the shock of impacts soon to come.

As for Reilly, he was their ungainly nursemaid in the armoury, spending hours checking weapons with each of them. He advised, demonstrated, cajoled and encouraged them in their waking nightmare. He deferred to Hurst without protest; regarded Hurst's toughest demands as a compliment. He was harbouring his own enormous viciousness for the future.

Jones remained taciturn, unchanging, almost a base line for reference. He was as taut as a piano wire but showed no sign of strain or fatigue. The rest of them, including Cooper, took good care not to provoke him in any way. They were thankful he was on their side.

Cooper, the youngest at twenty-two, had waded through too much blood in three years. He gave the impression he was becoming mentally exhausted. He had used up too much of his nervous resistance pretending he was not responsible for the carnage that had grown round him. It was symptomatic that he was the first to ask for sleeping pills. Hurst decided that one way or another this operation would be Cooper's last. He rejected the idea of altering his team at such a late and crucial stage, particularly as the chief psychologist assured him Cooper was still a long way from cracking up.

Harding had now found his place in the group and the group was beginning to accept him — on their terms not his. Hurst was content to note that Harding himself acknowledged the changes which had occurred, even though they were changes in him rather than shifts in his companions' uncompromising attitudes. Two particular incidents heightened Harding's new self-awareness.

The first incident took place one evening before dinner. He actually had a few minutes to spare and went to the bar to celebrate. The barman served him without commenting on the rarity of his appearance there. He sat by the fire and dozed over his sherry until joined by a quietly spoken middle-aged man who wanted to talk. After a few minutes desultory conversation the stranger remarked that he thought Harding had got himself mixed up with a pretty rough crowd.

Harding banged down his half-empty glass and left the bar, feeling his head would burst. Outside, in the hall, he had to stop and analyse this violent reaction to a harmless remark. He realised his pride was hurt by being singled out as not being one of the 'rough crowd', yet he was flattered by the implication he was mixed up with a special group. The comment had also touched a raw spot of self-pity, with the resultant need to confide in someone all the frustrations and humiliations of the last few weeks. This last effect doubly enraged him because it implied that the statement could be the start of an interrogation. He could no longer hold an innocent conversation outside the team with which he now wanted to be identified completely.

The second incident took place in the

team. They were all woken one night by a large force of enemy bombers grinding across the sky. The next morning, discussing the incident on the way to the range, Reilly asked Harding how soon he thought the enemy would be using the new explosive against Britain. Harding, thinking perhaps a matter of weeks and they'll only need to send one bomber, amazed himself by saying there was very little chance the Germans would get the explosive before we did. A month earlier he would have tried to shock them merely to assert his own superiority; now concern for them made him lie. He was protecting them from the devastation of a panic he himself could not escape: 'Christ in Heaven, let us get there in time!'

5

The next evening, when the five of them went to Hurst's room after dinner, they found it already occupied by the two men who had first interviewed Harding eight weeks ago.

'Ah, Brigadier,' said Hurst, ironically.

'Good evening, Alec. Excuse us letting ourselves in but your hostess thought it more discreet than waiting in the corridor.'

'Of course,' said Hurst, gruffly.

The general air of embarrassment increased when the visitors insisted on shaking hands with everyone. This forced friendliness irritated them, united as they were by a feverish anxiety to know the reason for this surprise visit.

The Brigadier suggested they all be seated so briefing could begin. Of course, there were not enough chairs so there was a further delay while Cooper was sent to his room to get some more. As soon as he had gone the Brigadier looked towards the closed door and then raised his eyebrows questioningly at Hurst. Hurst nodded. Harding, observing this by-play, correctly assumed the Major was being asked if he was happy about Cooper. No let out for poor old Cooper, thought Harding. He stared resentfully at the two visitors: the givers of life and death.

When Cooper came back with the chairs he was followed by two uniformed M.P.s carrying a large rectangular object covered with canvas. This they placed on the floor as directed by the Brigadier, while his companion, who had once more slipped into the lesser role, fussed about with chairs until they were arranged in a circle round the strange parcel. When the M.P.s had withdrawn everyone sat down. The two visitors sat next to each other and between Harding and Hurst. As the Brigadier looked round the circle the tense atmosphere closed on them like setting concrete.

'Gentlemen, we have come to put you in the picture. I am going to give you an introductory briefing now and there will

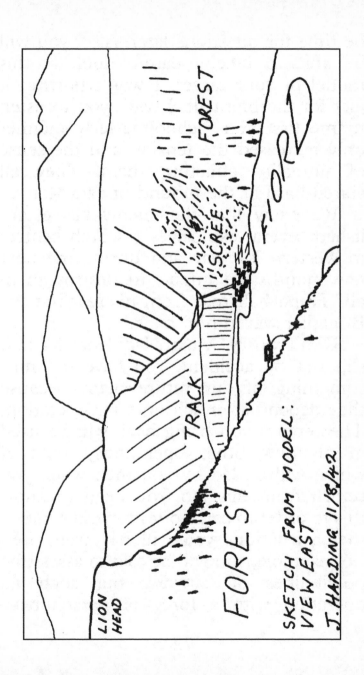

SKETCH FROM MODEL:
VIEW EAST
J. HARDING 11/8/42

LION
HEAD

FOREST

TRACK

SCREE

FOREST

FIORD

be time for questions later. Also, you will be able to take a careful look at this model of your target. I won't unwrap it just for the moment. I want you to listen to me first.' His schoolmasterly manner only increased the tension and the sense of unreality afflicting them. They all stared hard at the mound of canvas.

'We know that the enemy has established several explosives research centres in Western Norway and during the next few months we intend to destroy them all.' Hurst half rose from his seat but the Brigadier waved him back.

'Don't worry, Major. I did *not* let that slip out by accident. You have to know something of our future plans because they depend so much on your operation. The reports you bring back will be used in planning other operations, some of which will be led by you men when you return from this job. You need to know this in order to carry out properly some of the instructions you will be given later. For example, you will be told to assess the possibilities of carrying out such an operation with a force of parachutists.

This sort of assessment is most valuable.

'You already know you are not going on a simple search and destroy job; the collection of information is at least as important as destroying the target. Your team was built up with both these tasks in mind. Extra information which might be of value to the enemy has to be given you in this case. However, I see no reason for concern; this will simply encourage you to organise yourselves so as to eliminate the possibility of anyone being taken prisoner. You're used to that anyway.' He smiled coldly at Hurst.

'Your operation is 'Operation Wolf'. It has two objectives: (a) to discover precisely, repeat precisely, what the enemy is doing at a particular research station and (b) to destroy or help destroy that station. The first objective is more important than the second.

'The first objective is chiefly the responsibility of Captain Harding. The rest of you are to ensure he is able to inspect the research station from the inside. If Harding is unable to accomplish this task the rest of you will have to do the

73

best you can. However, Harding is the man with the knowledge and training to do the job properly so every effort must be made to protect him until his inspection is completed and he has reported back.

'The second task, that of destruction, will either be carried out by you or you will call in and direct an air attack. The R.A.F. regard the target as very difficult to hit but think they can do it if they have some help from the ground. This is one of the reasons why so much of your time has been spent on radio work.

'Your main handicap on this job is that you are going in late summer when the nights are still quite short. To compensate for this your party is a small one and can therefore operate from a base close to your objective. We cannot wait until the winter to send you, partly because the winter will be very tough and partly because we hope to complete all our other operations by the start of 1943. You have to go now. There is no alternative.

'Everything we are able to do to take the pressure off your area will be done. At the same time you must understand that what we *can* do is limited by the danger of arousing suspicion. We are going to step up dawn air attacks on coastal shipping and port facilities. These attacks will draw off German aircraft which might otherwise be patrolling your area. The R.A.F. will be most active on the three mornings after you land and this will help you when you may need help most; especially if you bump the enemy at your landfall. We dare not land you directly in the target area so you will have to make a cross-country journey. Empty skies at dawn will give you a better chance to find your bearings and go to ground for the day. Nevertheless, you cannot take what I have just said as being a guarantee of safety, especially as the night-fighter base at Bodo is being expanded. In addition, changeable and unpredictable weather may interfere with our plans.

'There is very little we can do on the ground to help you. However, as I think the Major explained, a number of small dumps of explosives and food have been hidden within easy reach of the target.

Here again, you cannot rely on this help; you may not be able to locate the dumps, especially if something happens to your guide. This means that you must carry sufficient equipment to do the job. Secondly, you will be helped and met by the guide I just referred to. He will be one of the two local men who managed to escape the enemy round-up.

'Apart from these limited forms of assistance I'm afraid you are on your own. That the majority of you are used to working in such circumstances was a major factor in determining your selection for this job.

'Now let's turn our attention to the target area and get down to details using the model.' He dragged the canvas from the lumpy object on the floor and they looked down at it; at the place where some of them would die.

It was a landscape of bleak, grim plateaux overlooking a deep, dark fiord. The east end of the fiord was shaped like a human foot with the toes pointing north. At the heel, on a small deltaic patch of lowland, stood a cluster of buildings. High above it a dam held back a long, narrow lake, the waters of which must formerly have fed the delta below. At the sides of the fiord the black, frowning cliffs rose almost vertically out of the water. These precipitous slopes led up to the high plateau country. Only in the east was there any variation in this pattern. There, the lake behind the dam lay in a deep groove in the plateau which extended eastwards to an area of high peaks looking down on peaceful, neutral Sweden. It was an escape route they would not be allowed to use.

'Ahem,' said the Brigadier. Their heads jerked up, concentration shattered. 'This excellent model will remain here so you can study it later. You will spend a lot of time sketching from it until you become familiar with all its features. However, there are some points we can consider straight away.

'One possible line of approach has been suggested by the Norwegians: this leads in from the north to this prominent rock face overlooking the fiord. This face is pock-marked by a series of caves and the whole thing is known as the 'Lion Head' because of its profile. The mouth of the 'Lion' is represented by a particularly large cave and from this point your attack could be launched. This cave is about three thousand feet above the water and about one mile from the enemy base on the opposite shore. The caves are easy to reach from the plateau but difficult to get to from below. They are also difficult to see from across the fiord, even though you will have an excellent view looking down.

'I don't want to discuss all these details now but I must point out that striking from a base on the opposite side of the fiord is not as difficult as you might think. This is because two of your caches of equipment have been placed on the south side of the water. However, you are not restricted in your choice of approach and some other line may strike you as more sensible when you get to the area.

'Now we believe this is a target worth investigating for several reasons. The buildings you see here, including the large dormitory block on the north side of the fiord, formed the Norwegian equivalent of a public school. It has its own H.E.P. station and is virtually a self-contained unit. When the Germans took over they told the local people the school would be used as a convalescent home for war wounded. Western Norway is a surprising choice of location for such an institution. Our suspicions were further aroused when a considerable amount of rebuilding was carried out. Part of the construction work was in the form of new extensions to old structures, the most interesting being the installation of another turbine and penstock. We would like to know why they need the extra power.

'Their next move was even more revealing. They rounded up every man and boy in this valley, and in the two adjacent valleys, and shipped them off as slave labour. The local men who had been forced to work on the school buildings were separated from their neighbours and relatives at the start of their journey to Oslo. They have not been heard of since. However, two partisans avoided the round-up and they were able to report further interesting facts. Firstly, only those three valleys were cleared of male population at that particular time, and secondly, as soon as the evacuation was complete, or rather when the Germans thought it was, an anti-submarine boom was constructed across the narrow mouth of the fiord. Yet this fiord only contains three small hamlets and the school; such extravagant precautions were more than enough to justify our suspicions.

'Your job is to find out what they are up to. We suspect either explosives or gas research. Captain Harding has already been working with you on what to look for if it is explosives. Starting tomorrow, he will also brief you on what to expect if they are working with gases.'

He smiled slyly at Harding as though making sure he realised who had been the power behind his transfer from atomic research. Harding just scowled back at him; words were pointless.

'Now gentlemen, let's have your questions.' He looked round at his class, waiting for someone to speak. The silence dragged on. Then Hurst came to his rescue.

'I understand the power supply is considered to be the weak link here. Can you elaborate on that for the rest of my group?'

'Certainly,' said the Brigadier, gratefully. 'Hydroelectric power is the only source of power for lighting, research, alarm systems and electrification of boundary fences — if they are electrified — we don't know that for certain. Anyway, we believe that if you first disrupt the supply of electricity you will neutralise their defences and cause chaos at the same time. To achieve this all you have to do is blow up the two pipes, or penstocks as they're called, which carry water down to the turbine house below the dam. This can easily be done by putting charges between the two pipes at the top where they lead away from the dam. The dam itself is outside the camp perimeter and is unguarded. You can walk along the top of it and place your explosive between the pipes.'

'How d'you know we can do that? Won't it need a lot of explosives?'

Cooper's questions were fired at the Brigadier.

'Oh, we've had a bit of luck with that problem.' He was almost apologetic. His companion handed him a sheaf of plans from his brief-case. 'These happen to be plans of the school. A quick-thinking teacher got them out as the Germans moved in. The dam and one penstock were built by a contractor from Trond-heim with the help of senior boys in the school; a sort of adventure project for engineering students. It is actually a very small and primitive affair, the dam being only twelve feet high and about twelve feet thick at the base. It is an earth dam with a concrete casing. The form of the lake floor, a very long but shallow depression, enabled them to store a lot of water without building a high dam. The second penstock added by the Germans did not demand that the dam be strengthened.

'It appears we can base our calculations of how much explosive you need on the information in these old plans. The answers we get suggest that you will be able to carry the right amount between you quite easily and, as an additional precaution, we've put twice that quantity into the caches we've set up. As for getting the charges between the pipes, we estimate this will take two of you about five minutes. We will show you how to position them for maximum effect but, with you and the Major as the explosives experts in your team, I doubt if you'll need much advice from us. The important point is not to get the wrong idea about this part of the operation; you are not trying to knock a hole in the dam, just trying to dislodge two pipes.'

This answer to Cooper's questions sparked off a great number of other questions and comments. It was not long before the circle of chairs was pushed aside and maps spread all round the room. The Brigadier and his assistant were subjected to a fierce, detailed cross-examination on every aspect of the operation until, after nearly two hours of discussion and argument, Hurst decided to end the briefing.

'I think we've enough material to work

on,' he said. 'What we need now is a little time to digest all the information we've just gained. I suggest we stop now and meet again later in the week.'

'Good idea,' said the Brigadier. 'We'll leave the model and maps here, so keep this room locked when you are out and put the papers in the house safe.

'I hope we have given you a clear introduction to your target. We'll go away now and leave you to it for a few days. We'll come back and see you later in the week just before you go. Good night to you all.'

The effect of his words was devastating. Breathlessly, they smiled weakly at each other. In that instant of time the last rivalries, the last contempts, were pushed aside by the realisation they needed each other in order to face the realities of the next few days.

★　★　★

A frenzy now possessed them. Everything had to be checked and double checked, every piece of equipment tested for the last time, every skill practised yet again. They needed the reassurance of their own competence. Fortunately, their fitness and shared sense of urgency now defeated exhaustion; the mental numbness and grit-eyed tiredness of their first days together did not repossess them; tension kept them constantly alert. Perhaps Cooper was right when he said they were too busy to be tired. But they were not too busy to think.

Their tenseness, their keener awareness of each other and of their group identity heightened their resentment of outsiders. They particularly resented the sudden appearance of well-wishers and busybodies foisted on them by various remote Ministry departments. These officious persons were at a disadvantage from the start since, except for Harding, all Hurst's team were more experienced than anyone who visited them. 'The Brig. and his fancy friend', as Jones called them were also treated with some curtness, and Hurst had to act as link and conciliator between the two factions. A petty detail of this rift was the resentment felt whenever the Brigadier tried to ingratiate himself by using their Christian names. They all accepted that Reilly was 'Joe' and Cooper was 'Andy', but no one thought of Hurst as 'Alec'! The Brigadier's attempts to be friendly merely resulted in his complete rejection. 'I wouldn't mind so much if the sod had to come wiv us,' snarled Cooper, speaking for them all.

The last major task was the careful packing of their rucksacks. Personal kit included sleeping bags, spare socks, medical kit and iron rations for five days. The bulk of their loads was made up of ropes, explosives, ammunition, weapons, the radio and radio spares. Cooper was to carry the radio and very little else, so he could afford to laugh as the rest of them each nervously packed twenty pounds of carefully wrapped explosive. Hurst said they didn't have to worry: the explosive was harmless by itself and he had the detonators in his pack. As long as he didn't blow up, the rest of them they were safe. They just looked at him, then went on packing.

When Hurst was satisfied their loads were as light as they could make them, they made up dummy packs of the same weights and carried them over the assault course. Then they repeated the exercise in pairs; each pair carrying three packs between them. Reilly and Harding were not pleased to observe that Jones and Cooper moved faster than they did.

'They think this is the bleedin' Royal Tournament,' growled Reilly from the bottom of the ditch. He climbed out scowling horribly.

A much happier expression appeared on his face when they went to the range for zeroing and final test firing. It was hard to tell which gave him the greatest pleasure: his companions' expertise or the perfect condition of their weapons. Even a last intrusion by the Brigadier failed to wipe the smile off his face.

The next afternoon, during a gentle work-out in the gym, Hurst was called away to the telephone. When he returned a few minutes later there was an odd expression on his face.

'That was the P.M. wishing us luck,' he said.

'Good God!' exclaimed Reilly. 'The old bulldog himself. That's never happened before.' Speechless, Jones and Cooper nodded agreement. Harding was also silent; he knew they were all sharing the same mixed feelings of pleasure and fear. The incident further underlined the vital importance of their operation.

That evening, without fuss or farewell, they departed. As the dusk of high summer crept round the house they were driven to the nearby aerodrome and put on a plane. Three hundred miles to the north a submarine lay motionless in cold Scottish waters, waiting to take them on the next leg of their journey.

PART TWO

The Scent

6

Anders Rogstad was cold, starving and frightened. Lying on the cliff top for the third successive night, he felt a little worse than on the previous night; the chill went a little deeper. He could no longer distinguish between fits of shivering induced by fear and those due to lack of warmth and nourishment.

Months of privation, living off a hard land had weakened him; fear for his family, fear for himself had sapped his resilience. His mind was beginning to break away from him, to drift off by itself. He was becoming two people, two exhausted strangers, meeting yet unable to succour each other. Only his family could help but he dared not ask them. His family. His family. 'Darling, darling, and little giant, love, Lars, love, if only. If only. If only you were away safe, safe somewhere, safe. It's not myself, myself, but family, dear family. Please God save them, look after them. Them! Help them to get away, get away!' A whimpering cry? His hands clutched at stones, burrowed into stones, skin bruised, skin torn. A cold grasp of panic. Had he been shouting again? Had he been crying out his fears, betraying himself and them? Was Sven right after all? Did he cry out? He looked nervously over his shoulder, sucking a raw finger at the same time.

All dark, all quiet. Only the sound of the sea. The irresistible sea surge; gentle, persistent, on and on like fear returning, returning in waves, always returning. No peace, no peace.

He stared down at the deserted beach two hundred feet below. The narrow band of silver sand gleamed under the bright moon; then cloud cut out the light and the beach vanished in the black shadows of the headlands. Only the distant sea remained coldly moonlit; a silver platter pitted and scarred with the dark stains of islands. Islands where perhaps others were doing the same . . . No! Not possible. No one else was doing what he had done. After eight months of sharing terror, of hiding, of supporting, of holding each other together, he had killed him. He had to do it, had to. Hysterical accusations and counter-accusations, each shrieking that it was the other who cried out in his sleep, betraying their hiding place. Sven was mad, crazy. Anders had forced him back, held him down, held the sacking across his face to stifle his cries, that was all. But when he was silent and the sack removed he was dead. Crying over the body, kicking it in rage made no difference.

When he could bear that dirty cave no longer he had crept away. He left the body lying there, he hadn't the strength to bury it. The stench, the staring eyes had not stayed in the cave but followed him, followed him to the sea's edge.

He stirred on his bed of sharp stones but could find no comfort. He looked at his watch: another hour to wait, then it would be too late. He would have to hide again and return for a fourth night. Perhaps they were coming now. He hoped the darkness would hide their arrival, that when the moonlight again swept the shore he would see a dinghy, or men, or footprints in the sand. He prayed for their safe arrival, for their success, yet dreaded the consequences of his prayers being answered. Success could only bring further agonies for his family and friends, while his own life would be even more at risk, his existence even more furtive and rat-like. He felt his patriotism being gnawed away by hunger, exhaustion and the continuous weight of fear. He had done so little himself but now help was on the way he could not welcome it wholeheartedly. Only the unthinking, the unimaginative, the unfeeling, find it easy to be brave, and he knew himself to be none of these things.

A black cloud slid greasily across the moon and once more the beach was hidden from him. For a moment he closed his eyes and rested his head on his arms. Perhaps he dozed for a few seconds, he never knew, but when he looked again towards the beach the flickering moonlight round the cloud edge revealed a large dinghy grounded in shallow water. As the light grew stronger he saw that two paddles had been placed in front of the dinghy in the form of a cross. They had landed.

A transitory excitement brought him to his feet, then caution and fear made him hesitate. There was something wrong with the scene on the beach: there were no footprints. He struggled with rising panic, rationalising the situation. They were experts, of course they would arrive silently and disappear quickly; there were no footprints because they had moved away along the water's edge. They must be hiding in the rocks at the end of the beach. But which end? He felt very conspicuous on the cliff edge and moved back. He watched the rocks at the south end of the beach where a cliff fall mantled the little strip of sand. He watched for more than a minute but saw no sign of life. He turned his attention to the northern headland with its rock strewn foot, but again no sign was given.

Five minutes passed. He sighed gently and began to walk down the cliff path. With every step he recalled the precise instructions he had been given: nothing to be said before the code words, expect five men on any one of four nights. He had not been given any names in case the enemy captured him before the landing. He was walking too fast, making too much noise. Why rush? They would wait. He had really seen the dinghy, hadn't he? Was he rushing to end his loneliness? He had been alone more than a month — ever since Sven.

Anders stepped on to the beach, stepped forward into bright moonlight. He picked up the paddles, keeping them crossed, and placed them in the dinghy. His movements were slow, careful, according to instructions. Each move kept him alive a little longer, each action was intended to reassure whoever was hiding toad-like among the green boulders thirty yards away. He stepped back from the dinghy, folded his arms and turned towards the southern headland. He stood, wetness behind weak knees, breathing heavily. Nothing happened. He wanted to run, to look round, to watch all directions at once, but he was rooted in the sands, unable even to turn his head. His mind began to drift out of his petrified body. He stood helpless in the fear-filled limbo of his indecision.

The viciousness of the challenge smashed the last brittle traces of his self-control. A great hand hugged him across the face, a knee drove into his spine and a knife was held across his throat. Someone laughed softly in his ear. He tried to speak, to give the password but could not. The knife was moved against his neck and he felt the sharp, acid pain of severed skin.

'Ease off, Sergeant. Ease off!' The voice came from beside him. The hand over his mouth jerked upwards, grasped his hair, wrenched his head back.

'Speak!' It was the man who held him.

'Steel Fire.' Anders dredged the passwords out of his receding consciousness.

He was immediately released, his knees folded and he fell forward on his face in the sand. No one offered to help him. He had endured to be treated like a dog. He deserved better than this. A slow rising anger began to permeate his crumbling mind. He struggled to his feet, tears of pain and rage on his cheeks. The shadowy figures of his attackers stepped back, stood poised, waiting. The Sergeant held the knife low at his side, the other man pointed a pistol at Ander's chest.

'You must forgive Sergeant Reilly,' said the gunman. 'He is rather too conscientious. I'm Major Hurst. You are Anders Rogstad.'

For an instant he wanted to deny his own identity, to do something to shake their brutal confidence. Then shock gave way to sense. He knew they would kill him at once if they had reason to doubt him. They were certainly used to killing those who got in their way. He knew this, not factually or by some logical reasoning, but through his dark intuition; perhaps the same intuition that had led him from his bed the night the Gestapo came for the men of his village. Intuition had saved him then and he thought it saved him now.

The first task, burying the dinghy, gave him time to rebuild some sort of composure. He and the Sergeant carried the paddles up the beach and began digging with them while the Major collapsed the dinghy and folded it into an untidy parcel. As they dug, Anders tried to calm his fears, to dispel feeble rage, to accept the idea that these men would be at his back from now on. As he considered this situation ugly doubts rose in his mind: he had expected five men; two could never accomplish the task. He could do little to help, he was too weak and too tired.

The irritation he had felt when first given his instructions and told almost nothing of his visitors returned afresh. Didn't the British realise what he was doing and risking for them? Why doubt him, why refuse to trust him completely? He was not even allowed to demand a password from them. It could be a trap for all he knew. He had seen the German words painted on the side of the dinghy. It could be a trick.

'Do we bury you here?' It was that animal of a Sergeant. Anders had stopped digging. 'Come on, get out of the way, dreamer, while we bury the dinghy.' He got out of the way and stood watching them. The dinghy was buried along with one paddle spade, the sand was smoothed over; the remaining spade was dismantled and put on to the Sergeant's pack. Somehow it was all reassuring.

'You lead the way but don't make as much noise as you did coming down,' said the Major.

'But are there no more of you? Can we do the job with just us three?'

'Us three?' mimicked the Sergeant.

'What job?' said the Major. 'Just lead on up the path will you.' He pushed him towards the base of the cliff. Immediately, three more shadows came swooping out of the blackness under the southern headland where they had been watching and waiting.

'Us three?' said Sergeant Reilly.

As Anders Rogstad climbed up the cliff path there was one thought, and one thought only, that gave him strength: it looked as though the British had learnt their lesson and were at last fighting like with like. The brave amateurs he had met in 1940 had not resembled these gruesome creatures. He almost felt sorry for the fresh-faced blond boys who strutted about his village, used his boat and lost his lines.

Just before they reached the top of the cliff he stopped. 'What's wrong now?' hissed the Sergeant. 'Feeling queer again?'

'I will speak with the Major.'

'What's up?' Major Hurst rose up out of the darkness below.

'Wait here while I see if all is clear.' Anders did not wait for a reply, just turned on his heel, dragged himself the last few yards and disappeared.

'Go with him, Joe,' growled Hurst. Fortunately, Anders did nothing that could have been misconstrued by his silent shadow, and when he returned to the cliff top he found all five visitors waiting where he had left them.

'Well?' said Hurst.

'All is clear I think.'

'You think? That's not good enough for us.'

Anders replied by sitting on the nearest boulder and putting his head in his hands. From a great distance, beyond the noises in his head, beyond the whisper of the sea on the sand, he heard the men muttering. Then one of them walked over to him.

'Here, you. Drink this!' A hand on his shoulder felt the worn cloth, the shrinking flesh, his trembling as he choked on the raw spirit. 'Better?'

He nodded and struggled to his feet. His humiliation was complete. He would never bring himself to speak the carefully rehearsed words of welcome which he had saved up for daybreak. He had nothing to offer these men. Slowly and carefully he said: 'I am now ready.'

He led them into the hills, walking as fast as his strength allowed, but they had no difficulty in keeping up with him; their heavy packs and weapons did not slow them, nor did marching in darkness across strange terrain. When they rested they gave him food and a hot drink from a vacuum flask. They still had work for him to do.

The party moved on again, even faster now dawn threatened. Several times Anders looked over his shoulder to see if he had outstripped the others, but they were always there, at intervals of ten yards, weapons ready, moving silently after him. Eagerly, suspiciously, they tracked him, tensed for the kill. A pack of wolves could not have been more horrifying, snapping at his heels as he tried to outdistance them in a frightful nightmare from which he was never to awake.

So he led them into his country, into his mountains; a party of killers who would fester in the hills until it was time for them to break out and slaughter everyone in their path.

7

By daybreak they were ten miles from the coast and had climbed to the high plateau about four thousand feet above sea level. This high surface stretched before them like a featureless plain, an endless waste of rock and coarse turf, apparently offering no place of concealment. But as they advanced, the level surface revealed itself to be gently undulating; a series of small rises and depressions, the edges of which were mantled by sheets of boulders. One such boulder field was so extensive, and the boulders in it so large, that it suggested itself as a good hiding place. They turned into the maze of rocks and soon found a camp site: a small patch of ground with boulders about five feet high on three sides of it. 'Will this do?' asked Hurst. Anders nodded.

In the strengthening light they inspected each other carefully, and Hurst introduced each member of his team to the Norwegian. Anders saw the same man five times, the same single-minded ruthless soldier stared back at him from five different faces. The Captain differed from the others in ways Anders could not define, although he received the same gruff greeting from him as from the others. Cooper and Jones also found it difficult to speak to him, while Reilly and Hurst returned his resentful stare with a calculating look that turned his knees to water. In the cold dawn light he found them all even more frightening than at their first encounter. Nothing in their attitudes suggested which of them had offered him that drink at the cliff top. He wondered if he had imagined it.

His visitors were not impressed by him and did not pretend otherwise. They saw not a tall, blond Viking but a short, dark, long-haired man, grey-faced and shaking with fatigue. So deeply were the marks of strain and starvation embedded in his face it was impossible to guess his age. Except for the bloodstain on his collar, his thin, weather-worn clothes were clean and neatly patched, but, like the man, they were slowly rotting away.

Hurst began rapping out orders. He did not waste breath on their exhausted guide but sent Cooper and Jones out as scouts while Reilly and Harding constructed a simple shelter in the rocks.

Cooper and Jones moved off in opposite directions, striding quickly towards the ill-defined horizon where the grey ground merged into the flat backcloth of low cloud. Into this barren, featureless distance both men suddenly disappeared. Harding was amused by the expression of disbelief on Anders' face; although his expression might equally have been the result of looking at the primitive shelter Harding and Reilly were constructing.

They had stretched ground-sheets between the tops of the largest boulders, fixing the edges with heavy stones. This gave them a roughly rectangular shelter with stone walls on three sides and a sagging waterproof roof. One side was left open. When it was completed no one volunteered to go inside. They stood and looked at it; they would be very cold and damp by the end of the day.

'I suppose we've got to stay here?' said Reilly.

'I am much afraid we must,' said Anders. 'As you can see there is not much shelter up here and we do not want to be caught in the open by air patrol.'

'Can we brew up now?' asked Reilly.

'Is that all right, Anders?' said Hurst.

'I am sorry?' Anders was apologetic. Harding wondered if it was the words he did not understand or if he was astonished that Hurst used his first name.

'Brew up, use our stove?'

'Oh, I understand. Yes it will be safe for one more hour.'

'Good. But I think we'll wait a little while for Jones and Cooper.'

'Couldn't we fill the flask for them?' asked Harding. Now they had stopped work he was shivering.

'That's not what I meant. I want to hear them report first, don't I?'

Anders looked from one to the other, sensing some past antagonism rising to the surface. Then he frowned. 'I see. You think I do not know what is safe in my own home country?'

107

'No, not at all. It's just that I feel we must take all precautions. I'm not mistrusting your judgement at all.' Hurst's sympathetic tone pacified the Norwegian but had a quite different effect on Harding and Reilly. As the two of them unpacked the stove Reilly muttered: 'Our friend had better watch out for the Major, he's playing Father Christmas. That's always a danger signal.' Suddenly drawn to the Sergeant by this little conspiracy Harding smiled at him and nodded, although he was not quite sure what he meant. Reilly knew that Hurst's mind was blocked with the problem of what to do with their guide; he also knew the solution Hurst must eventually accept. Had this knowledge been Harding's also he would not have smiled and nodded so cheerfully.

When Cooper and Jones returned, satisfied no one else was in the area, breakfast was cooked and quickly eaten.

By 06.00 hours Jones and Reilly were out of sight half a mile away, while the rest of them, having concealed all outward signs of the camp were wrapped in their sleeping bags. Soon, all the men in the makeshift tent were asleep except Anders. In spite of having a full stomach for the first time in months, and in spite of the warmth of the sleeping bag borrowed from Reilly, his distraught mind kept him awake. It was grappling with the fact of these strangers being with him; trying to equate their presence with the desperate futility of his own private war. His war, a war of inaction, of separation and loneliness, of shadows of lost friends, a private war ruled by the towering, accusing figure of Sven, conflicted with the new, harshly lit world of action and teamwork these men brought with them.

At last he did sleep, a deep dead sleep undisturbed by the shadows that usually brought him awake, sweating and raving.

He woke as Jones and Reilly blundered into the tent. He sat up and saw Hurst and Cooper just disappearing into the mist now settling on the plateau. He looked at his watch: it was 10.00 hours; he had slept for four hours. Reilly and Jones, cursing the cold, dived into the two empty sleeping bags. Reilly shook his head when Anders made a move to get out of his bag. Harding smiled at the confused Norwegian.

'It's all right. We've just changed guards. Hurst and Cooper are on watch now. I suppose I'm next. I don't know about you.'

'Do not worry. I will awake again if required.'

But he was not required and neither was Harding. Hurst was absolutely firm about that when he returned. 'Neither of you will take part in guard duties today, or any other day. We can't afford an accident to either of you, at least not yet.' His words and mirthless smile incensed Anders who felt he was not trusted to do the job properly. When he remonstrated with him Hurst closed his eyes and pretended to be asleep, leaving Harding to placate their guide. He calmed him down as well as he could and tried to explain that Hurst dare not risk the life of their guide while they were walking towards the target area.

Anders was not convinced; his original feelings about his visitors were growing in strength. He was marked down as expendable if that became necessary; in fact, he wondered if necessity would enter into it. They were all so tough, fit and confident that he felt he was a passenger and as such might be disposed of the instant Hurst decided he could manage without him. He could not claim for himself the same mysterious immunity, the same protection, as could the Captain.

'You do not mind being treated this way?' he asked. Harding stared at him, knowing he was not asking the question he wished to ask.

'Not really,' he replied. 'I know this part of the operation will not demand much of me. My effort will be made later. Meanwhile, I'm quite happy to accept any arrangements which make life easier for me.'

'I thought you British were prideful.'

'That's not quite the word, but I understand your meaning. But pride has nothing to do with it. I can say this now but it took me several painful weeks to learn the lesson. Perhaps you should laugh at us a little, it might help.' His words were meant kindly but made little impression on the indignant Norwegian.

'But they treat you like a prisoner. Last night on the climb up here you are in the middle of the party and always the Sergeant or the Major keep next to you. Of course, it is so different for me, I must become used to working in a group again. But it is strange when all of us do not share the same work.'

'I can understand how it appears to you, but remember you have an important job to do for us; you need to be as fit and rested as possible.' Anders opened his mouth to protest but Harding cut him short. 'You must have had a pretty rough time since you escaped the round-up. It is only fair you are not driven as hard as the rest of us. This is a grim country to survive in for nearly a year.' Fortunately, this remark deflected Anders' attention.

'Yes, that is true. I have no wish to have another year like this one. It is particularly hard for me knowing my wife and child are near but I cannot help them in any way. Sometimes I do not feel more fortunate than my friends who were carried off by the Nazis. I know that is stupid but it is like living with — with a temptation.' He bit into his lip, lay back on his bed and stared up at the grey roof of their rough tent. Harding was embarrassed and said the first thing that came into his head.

'Your child was not taken away then?'

'No. My boy, Lars, is too young even for the Nazis to work to death. He is four years old.'

'Is that all?'

Anders turned to face him and smiled suddenly. 'Why Englishman, how old do you think I am? Come make a guess.'

Harding was feeling more and more uncomfortable. He looked into his companion's face, made a guess, knocked off five years and said: 'Forty-five or six perhaps?'

Anders stopped smiling. 'I am thirty-three.' He closed his eyes, turned on to his side and muttered: 'As you say — a hard country.'

By late afternoon the mist had thickened considerably and Hurst brought his sentries back to within one hundred yards of the camp. Anders was not worried by the reduced visibility but Hurst pretended that *he* was. He made the Norwegian trace out their route on his maps, but without actually marking them in any way in case they fell into the wrong hands. Hurst also made him indicate the exact locations of the caches of equipment which he had helped to hide some weeks earlier.

Then Hurst asked him when they would be meeting the other partisan who had dodged the Germans. Anders did not reply. Cooper and Harding stared at him. They knew something was badly wrong even before Anders' face began to pucker. Intuitively, Hurst knew he could not let the question pass unanswered and he repeated it. They were all shocked by the result.

Anders began to laugh; a soft, hair-raising chuckling noise. 'Never, never! Sven is dead. I killed him.'

'Why?' asked Hurst, hoping the brutal question would check the man's hysterical laughter.

'He talked in his sleep.' Anders laughed

feebly and began sucking his fingers.

'You thought it necessary?' said Hurst, very quietly.

Anders nodded. The first tears rolled down his face. Harding watched, speechless. Behind him Cooper softly muttered: 'The poor, poor sod. He's finished.'

This time Harding fully understood the minds of his companions. He also knew the futility of making any comment of his own.

The unbearable tension was broken by Anders himself. He wiped a hand across his face, muttered something in Norwegian and crawled out of the tent. He sat just outside and muttered to himself. The three men looked at each other.

'I don't think the poor devil's going to be much help to us, Major,' said Cooper, at last. Hurst shrugged his shoulders helplessly; he was obviously as shaken as the rest of them. 'We'll see soon enough now. Let's get dinner.'

This time the meal was taken in shifts so that guard duties were not interrupted. Hurst and Harding persuaded Anders to eat with them while Cooper waited for the other two. The Norwegian was silent at first, looking sullenly at his plate out of eyes strangely blank, strangely glazed. However, the food appeared to work some gentle miracle and by the end of the meal he had relaxed sufficiently to join in the halting flow of conversation. The result was catastrophic.

Hurst happened to mention it was Friday and Anders added: 'It is also what I call wife day.'

Hurst stared at him. Harding put down his fork. Cooper stopped fiddling with the primus. At last:

'Why wife day?' asked Hurst.

'I usually see my wife on Fridays.' Complete silence again, the mist brushing silently against the tent roof, the empty plateau listening.

'Explain please. How do you see your wife on Fridays? Who else knows of this?' Stone words falling.

'It is not really a meeting,' said Anders, suddenly terrified. 'It is just she walks in our meadow with our child in the afternoon and, if I am near, I watch her through my binoculars. That is all. I swear that is all.' They stared at him for a long time.

'Oh, God,' whispered Harding. He could imagine the woman standing there, giving and drawing strength from the knowledge that this man, this wreck of a man she would not recognise, a man she never saw, was watching her. It was pathetic, tragic, hideous. The simple act illuminated all the terror and agony of existence under enemy occupation. If Hurst was similarly affected he gave no sign of it.

'Are you sure no one else knows of this?' he asked.

'I am sure.' Anders spoke more firmly.

'I do hope you're right. I hope you're bloody well right.' He banged his fist on the ground, his face darkened alarmingly. 'Don't you understand what you've done? If anyone else has any idea about this they'll wonder why you are not there today. Never mind about how well you hide, it's all another stupid, bloody risk. And we knew nothing about it. My God! Why can't you people understand what total war is. All this play acting makes me puke!'

He crawled out of the tent followed by Cooper, leaving Harding to make peace once more. But there was nothing he could say; even to apologise for Hurst's unfeeling final remarks was a waste of time. Anders and Hurst were so far apart as men, so far apart in experience they would never understand each other. For one man months of thorough preparations were at risk because of a sentimental peasant; while the other man, able to continue his war only because he knew his family was alive, could not see beyond Hurst's brutish exterior.

As soon as Reilly and Jones had been fed Hurst gave orders to break camp. No one was sorry. The tent was uncomfortable in more ways than one; the pungent odours of perspiration, primus fumes and damp clothing were as unpleasant as having too much time to think.

They moved out, leaving no trace of their stay, and set off at the same fast pace as on the previous night. They did not wait for darkness but, using the mist as cover, made an early start to the march. They moved in single file as before:

Anders Rogstad leading, then Reilly, Hurst, Harding, Cooper and Jones. Because of the mist they walked close together so that the leader was always in sight of the last man.

In the early morning they arrived at the plateau edge overlooking a mist-filled valley. In spite of their weariness they all felt the same sudden stirring of excitement. The valley at their feet was the one next to that containing the target. Once they had crossed it and climbed back to the plateau on the other side they would be less than two hours march from the Lion Head.

8

They stood poised on the plateau edge, peering nervously down into the mist-choked valley.

'Wait a minute,' said Hurst. 'There's barely an hour to go before full light. Do we hide up here, or have you got a better idea?'

'It is — all — right,' gasped Anders, struggling to get his breath. 'I have been here before. About four — four hundred metres below is an abandoned *saeter* — summer pasturing with some old huts. No one ever climbs to it now. It is safe. We can rest.' He swayed on his feet as he spoke. He needed the rest most of all.

'I don't like the idea of huts,' growled the Major. 'It'll be one of the first places they'll check if Jerry suspects someone's moving across this bit of country. It will be easy to pick out from the air as well, once the mist clears. Why are you so sure it's safe?'

'The place is hard to reach from below. It is high above the forest edge, so it is not seen from the valley. This part of the valley is poor land, good only for trees, so there is not a village or farm near. I know this because my home is not far.'

'Maybe so. Is there anywhere else?'

Anders hesitated, looked at his feet, muttered something to himself.

'What?' barked Hurst.

'There is only our little cave, too small for all you.' He paused, then: 'Sven is there.' He shuffled his feet.

'That needn't stop us,' said Hurst, crudely.

'I will not take you.' Anders giggled suddenly and put his fingers in his mouth. His black, sunken eyes glazed over. No one knew what to do. Then he giggled again, a hideous sound. Hurst shook his head sadly, stepped up to him and slapped him viciously across the face. Anders staggered and fell down. Hurst kicked him in the ribs and ordered him to get up.'

'Leave him,' snarled Hurst, as Harding stepped forward.

Speechless, Harding watched Anders struggle to his feet. This man had been faced with a free choice: to escape or stay, and he had volunteered to stay. Unlike Harding, he had made his decision without being pressured into it. That decision was ruining his mind and health. Now he had his reward — a blow in the face. Harding's lip curled as he scowled at Hurst. The Major glared back at him, daring him to express the feelings which disfigured his face. But Harding said nothing; there was no point now that the trap was closed round him. He knew all his companions were tainted with a similar madness and there was nothing he could do about it.

Hurst was as angry with himself as with Anders. Striking the man was unavoidable, but he knew the strength of the blow had been determined more by his own feelings of frustration than by the need to steady the Norwegian. Like Harding, he felt himself to be surrounded by madmen; but they were madmen who would jeopardise the whole operation for reasons totally irrelevant to the desperate task in which they were all involved. That bloody young fool of a scientist had been on the point of splitting the party just then. He swore under his breath and looked at Anders. There was no point in driving him to lead them to the cave; it might be too small and he would probably go completely crazy before he got there. It was a pity that the mist made it necessary to use the man for the next few hours however much he slowed them down.

Anders looked into his face and, with the clarity and perceptiveness given to those at the edge of the pit, saw everything that was in the Major's mind. For a moment they were too close for words to be necessary. Then they could no longer meet each other's eyes.

'Well,' said Hurst, softly, 'the huts it is then. Lead the way, Anders. We'll be right behind you but don't try to rush things, we don't want to blunder into someone in this ruddy mist.'

Cautiously, they crept down the valley side, following the shambling, shaking figure of their guide. They walked in single file, two yards apart, so that no one would lose contact with the rest of the party. They tried to move silently but their breathing, their hesitant footsteps, the creaking of straps as a pack was adjusted, were like shouts of betrayal that echoed and re-echoed between the grey walls surrounding them. As they moved down into the pit of enveloping, thickening mist it brushed against them leaving a sparkling slime on everything. They became obsessed by a passion for wiping off this clammy touch from faces, weapons and clothes. As the slope steepened they were convinced they were being drawn down to a death fall over vertical cliffs; they leaned backwards as they moved, took shorter steps, moved more slowly. It became difficult to focus their eyes on any one object; large boulders crept up to surround them, a ruined cairn sprang from the mist, threatening to topple on to them. The mist itself became a living thing, twisting up towards them, grasping thighs, arms, throats, pulling them down, drowning them in its soft, deceitful, inescapable folds.

They had lurched down about a thousand feet of that interminable hillside when the movement of the mist suddenly increased. It began to boil, to swirl away from them. There was not much time left before it would sink away into the valley, leaving them exposed on the high slopes. 'Almost there,' gasped Anders. The words came distorted, hissing towards them. They might have been a signal.

Immediately the mist lifted.

They stood paralysed on a steep, grassy slope without shelter of any kind. Confused and disoriented they blinked in bewilderment as the mist rolled back from them faster than they could run. A hundred yards ahead of them were revealed some ruined huts and, beyond them, the green spears of conifers on the lower valley side. The sharp light of dawn poured over the hillside. 'Get into the trees!' barked Hurst.

They ran forward but none of them reached shelter.

As Harding and Reilly drew level with the huts they came face to face with a sleepy, half-dressed soldier emerging from a doorway to stretch his cramped legs. As his jaw dropped Reilly's first shot splintered into his forehead. Harding was knocked to the ground by Hurst as the Major plunged into the nearest hut. A staccato burst of machine-gun fire within the hut was matched by shooting on the far side of the clearing as Jones fell to the ground and opened fire. The roof of another hut erupted in flame and flesh as Reilly hurled a stick grenade through the open window. Harding, lying winded, fumbling for the safety catch of his gun, watched appalled, as bewildered, half-wakened, half-dressed grey figures came staggering into the open, clutching at torn chests and stomachs, and jack-kniving on to their faces. The noise was deafening: Schmiessers hammering, bullets screeching off stone and bone, cries of agony, someone sobbing, a man coughing to death in blood and cordite fumes.

A moment of silence, then single shots, deliberate, unhurried shooting into every torn, trembling body. Harding was never to forget the look of concentration on Jones's face as he shot both dead and dying through the head. He was paying some personal debt absolutely beyond Harding's comprehension. The echoes of those single shots were hurled back by the valley walls until shots and echoes smashed into the ears of the dying in a great dawn chorus. Harding closed his eyes.

Hurst towered over him, prodded him with his toe. 'Get up. I'm glad to see you had the sense to stay down while we were working. Your turn comes later.' He grinned ironically at him then swung round as Reilly and Cooper ran from the woods below giving thumbs-up signs. 'All accounted for,' shouted Reilly.

'They were only here for summer camping,' said Anders, coming out of the nearest hut. 'They were camping.' His face was yellow and his hands shook. 'They were only camping. Here are their orders, you see.' He held out blood-stained papers.

'So what?' said Jones, breathlessly.

'So his good advice was useless,' snarled Cooper. 'Now the fat's really in the fire.'

'Shut up!' ordered Hurst.

They stood and looked at each other, then turned to watch the mist slipping still further into the trees, exposing yards and then miles of timbered hillside. Far away to the west there was a muffled explosion, then curving up out of the mist came a deep red Very light, flaring high over their heads, then fading, dying, plunging back to the mist-shrouded valley floor.

'That's that. They'll get no reply from up here,' said Reilly. 'My grenade blew up the radio as well as the operator and we haven't missed a single Jerry. I've checked every hut.' He turned on the Norwegian. 'What now little man?'

'I know these men,' said Anders. He blurted out the information as though speaking against his will. He gestured helplessly with his hands at the corpses huddled on the steep hillside.

'Do you?' said Hurst. Harding shook his head in astonishment. Why this quiet, conversational tone? No recriminations?

'Yes,' said Anders. 'They are some of Stampf's men. I escaped from them a few weeks ago.'

'Did you really?' said Hurst, politely. 'No one told me you'd ever been captured. Is that what you meant?'

'Yes.' The answer was given reluctantly.

'Their friends down in the valley might recognise you then?' Hurst sounded bored.

'Yes.'

Hurst shot him between the eyes at a range of three feet. The body was thrown backwards by the force of the bullet. Something cracked against the side of the hut behind it and a thick, red smear began to creep down the stonework.

Deafened by the explosion they looked down on what was left of their guide — a small, shrivelled figure at their feet. Then they turned to Hurst: Cooper blinking in astonishment, Jones's face expressionless, but with his hands to his side as though he had felt the blow from that bullet, Reilly stoney-faced, already knowing the simple explanation. All this Harding saw in the instant he heard his own voice beginning to shout: 'But he didn't betray us. He didn't know the Germans were here. You can see that. You can tell they weren't expecting us.' His voice rose to a shriek.

'He wasn't a traitor, just an encumbrance,' stated Hurst.

The simple answer cut away all Harding's rage, disposed of all his protests. This death was the climactic horror, a greater disaster than their discovery and the one-sided slaughter that followed. He looked round appealingly at a ring of stone faces, desperate for any explanation, however mad, that would make this thing come right. They looked at him thoughtfully, then turned back to Hurst.

'Jerry mustn't know we did this. Collect as many weapons and pairs of boots as you can carry. Our only chance now is to convince them this is the work of partisans.' Then he turned on Harding. 'Wake up sonny. Partisans are short of boots aren't they? We're leaving them a real, dead, known partisan to convince them. Don't stand there gaping. Get some boots!'

Harding fell on his knees beside the nearest grey-clad figure, a young corporal with his chest blown away. He undid the boy's boots and tried to pull them off, but one of them stuck fast. In rage and disgust he wrenched at the foot and the corpse writhed at such brutal treatment. Harding shuddered. He was now utterly lost in a black, confusing maze of rage and terror; everything he saw and touched was blotted out by recollections of the face of Anders Rogstad. He looked over his shoulder to where the Norwegian's body lay, just as Hurst rolled it over so he could search the back pockets. The gaping hole in the back of the head explained what had been thrown against the wall by the force of the shot.

'You murdering bastard!' He found himself standing over Hurst, without knowing how he got there. 'I'll make sure you pay for this.'

Hurst grinned mirthlessly at him. 'Such language doesn't go with an Oxford accent, John. And while you're cursing me don't forget the man's family. When Jerry recognises this fellow they'll be after his wife and kid. *Don't do that*!'

He knocked Harding's gun to one side.

Harding, suddenly aware of what he had meant to do, dropped both gun and boots on to Anders' body.

Hurst handed him back his gun. 'Pull yourself together! Don't let the others see you like this. Do you really think I enjoy this, you self-righteous shit? What's the matter with you, anyway? You know better than any of us what's at stake, so why all the melodrama? Just set a few Norwegians against the population of London, will you?' He got to his feet and looked down at Anders. 'Poor old devil. If ever a man talked himself to death he did.' He sighed. 'Well, let's go.'

Guiltily, Harding watched him walk across the clearing. He could not admit he owed the Major any sort of apology, not with Anders' body at his feet. He stooped down, rolled the body on to its back and stretched out his hand to close the eyes. He couldn't do it. The eyes had rolled up and flooded with blood. He couldn't touch them. 'Nothing I can do for you,' he muttered. Then in the same moment knew there was something he could try to do. He ran after the Major who, hearing his hurried steps, turned warily to face him. 'Major, wait!'

'Yes?' The steely eyes looked through him again. Harding knew he was wasting his breath, this man knew what he meant to say before he opened his mouth, but he had to speak out, to try to reach him.

'I suppose there's no way of warning his wife?' He was ashamed of the feeble phrasing.

'Why?' unhelpfully.

'Perhaps she could get away before the Germans find out about all this.' He waved an arm vaguely towards the piled bodies.

'Not a chance! How could we find her? Where would she go? Her only hope is that Jerry doesn't know about Rogstad's family or doesn't know he's a local man. Or if they guess he's a local, then no one gives the game away by identifying him.'

'But if she doesn't even know?'

'So what?'

'Well what I mean is — well, she'll go on walking out in the meadow every Friday.'

'Like the figures under one of those

chiming clocks, you mean? A sort of yo-yo?'

Harding could only look at him, revolted by the grotesque images conjured up by this last monstrous remark. Hurst stared back. Then in a milder voice, 'Sorry, John, that's how it is. Now come on, we've a job to do. Let's make a success of it for Anders' sake.'

The nauseating insincerity of this remark had little effect on Harding when compared with the revulsion he felt as the Major patted him on the shoulder. He could not prevent himself cringing. Hurst's face darkened, then he shrugged and turned away. With Harding trailing behind him, he walked across to the other three men who eyed them curiously but asked no questions. They were standing in line, and as Harding walked towards them he half-expected them to line up their guns on his chest. Alienation was complete.

The moment passed. He was too valuable, they had to keep him alive whatever else happened. They were all mad of course, but he had to make sure he kept control of his mind. The Major waited for Harding to join the group before he explained the next move.

'Not only must we avoid capture and try to hide the fact we're not local men, we must also avoid giving away our objective. We'll move out of here as fast as we can and keep moving as long as there's no air search laid on. We move east along this valley and away from the target area. We must convince Jerry we're going to cross into Sweden, then when we've done that we can double back and circle round to the Lion Head. Any questions?' There were no questions. 'Well, let's go!'

They left the silent, desolate clearing, with its shattered huts and its green grass mottled red and grey, and plunged into the deeper, darker green of the trees. The forest was not continuous at that altitude so they several times emerged from it to cross broad stretches of grass or bare rock scree. Their extra loads of arms and boots weighed them down and the steep slopes along which they picked their way put a tremendous strain on ankle and calf muscles. In spite of their fitness, they were soon soaked in perspiration and, as the sun rose higher, they began to look forward to arriving at the next patch of cool, sheltering woodland; even the stunted conifers at the tree line were a welcome alternative to sun-soaked ankle-straining scree.

At long last Hurst halted at the edge of a clearing and waited for the others to join him. They arrived one by one, with Jones at the rear, bathed in sweat and breathing heavily. The Major's fierce pace, relentlessly maintained for nearly two hours, had fully extended them for the first time. If Anders had been with them such a high speed would have been unthinkable. They shrugged off their packs and sprawled under the twisted trees. Hurst did not let them rest for long but made them pile up half the captured weapons and boots and cover them with a large mound of stones. 'Jerry won't miss that. It'll convince them they're on the right trail,' said Hurst.

Even as he spoke there was a new, dramatic development in the situation.

From far below them, on the valley floor, came the sound of a powerful engine. Hurst sprang into the open with field glasses ready.

'They've got some sort of half-track down there. They're using the old forestry road to beat us to the valley head. This is our chance to convince them they've got the right idea. Pick up your kit and run across the next clearing to that clump of trees. I want them to see you go, so run fairly slowly and look as tired as you can.'

'That bit's easy,' growled Cooper, swinging three pairs of boots over his shoulder and breaking into a gentle trot. As the others followed they looked down into the valley, now free of mist. Some three thousand feet below they could make out the sinuous line of the old road disappearing and then reappearing in the trees; moving jerkily along it was a tractor-like machine large enough to carry several men. They halted in the trees and waited for Hurst to join them.

'Well done. I watched them through the glasses as you ran across the clearing. I'm pretty sure they saw you. There was a great deal of movement with a lot of arm waving. They'll soon stop that when they reach the end of the track and have to climb up towards us.'

'How many?' asked Reilly.

'About a dozen I think. Roughly the same number we bumped earlier.'

'Are we going to fight them off?' asked Cooper.

'No. I want us to keep out of range from now on, just give them sufficient encouragement to keep the scent warm. Let's get on. A little faster I think, now you've less to carry. Five minutes rest in about an hour.'

He again set a blistering pace which soon had them strung out over a quarter of a mile. To everyone's surprise it was Jones who found the going toughest; he was particularly uncomfortable on scree, and at one point missed his footing and rolled about thirty feet down the slope. However, he shrugged off all offers of help except Cooper's; he let him carry his share of the captured equipment.

When they next rested, in another stand of trees, Hurst made a second cache of weapons and boots, leaving the party with only their original loads to carry. In spite of this off-loading, he allowed them to rest a little longer than the promised five minutes and watched thoughtfully as Jones drank the last of the water in his bottle. He made no comment when Jones handed the bottle back to him. They all knew they had waited nearly five minutes before Jones arrived, in spite of the fact Cooper had been carrying his extra load for him since he fell on the scree.

As they rested, looking out from their cool, green cave of shade, Hurst pointed out the next part of their route. They were almost at the end of the valley and, in order to regain the level of the high plateau, they would have to climb fairly steeply as they moved east. The main obstacle before them was represented by a great white scar running down the valley side and reaching to the valley floor. There was no way round it. It was difficult to tell exactly what it was at that distance but they could see it had cut a broad path through the forest beneath them. 'Looks like a new avalanche track,' said Reilly, lowering the glasses. 'It certainly went through those trees without any trouble. Watch your step when you get on to it, there may be a lot of very loose rocks there.'

'One good thing about it: a half-track can't climb it,' said Hurst.

9

The dirty white scab of the rock fall lay before them. As they approached this intimidating barrier it appeared to be an impenetrable maze of white boulders; its terrifying complexity the result of millions of tons of rock being torn out of the plateau edge and hurled down into the deep, green valley. While still half a mile away they began to feel its strength through the force of refracted sunlight spiking into their faces. In the midday heat every step forward was accompanied by a whitening of the boulders, a multiplying of silvered surfaces embedded in the freshly carved avalanche track.

Half-suffocating in the heat of the open hill slopes they had long ago removed anoraks and sweaters. Now they had also to endure this piercing reflection slashing at them head high across the withered turf of the valley side. With hunched shoulders, bowed heads and half-closed eyes they fought their way eastward and upward, while the relentless sun climbed over them until, poised at their shoulders, it burnt directly into the side of the rock fall facing them. Thus, driven from behind by the sun on their backs, they were forced into the dazzling wall of sun-soaked rocks.

There were other pressures to endure. The faint, muffled noises of their hasty progress eastwards were several times overwhelmed by louder, fiercer sounds of straining engines rising out of the valley below them: the constant reminder of pursuit. The fluctuating volume of engine noise echoed strangely from the tree-shrouded lowland, and from time to time the shriek of ill-managed gears falsely raised their hopes. They knew the valley track was a far longer, more tortuous route than theirs, but ignorance of relative speeds only confused their calculations; moments of optimism gave answers which were encouraging; then a more pessimistic arithmetic hinted at disaster and they almost reversed their flight.

The open skies also intimated disaster. All morning they had expected enemy aircraft to attack them but the skies remained empty and silent. The early morning air attacks on coastal shipping had drawn every aircraft away from their area; but a few R.A.F. planes, operating almost at the limit of their range, could not be expected to engage the Luftwaffe for very long. There would soon begin a desperate race between refuelled, rearmed aircraft and the slowly growing clouds above the high ground. The prize was their lives but they could only wait helplessly for the outcome.

The greatest pressure of all, the greatest threat, came from within: the inexplicable failure of Corporal Jones. It was his halting progress that held them back while their enemies leapt ahead; that left them exposed to the inevitable air search. They were too often halting and waiting for precious minutes while Jones trailed slowly across the steep slopes leading to the rock fall. Neither threats nor offers of help brought any response. Hurst, already blaming himself for letting his party blunder into disaster, was now desperate to preserve at least some part of his force. Must he now kill Jones as he had the Norwegian, and for the same reasons?

At last they rested in the inadequate shade of two stunted trees; their last rest before climbing on to the rocks. They arrived, one by one, collapsing in the shade and struggling to regain their breath. When Jones caught up with them he slumped to the ground with his back against a tree. Unlike the others, he had not removed his anorak and, although sweating heavily, still did no more than loosen his collar with his left hand. His right hand he kept pressed against his side as though he was badly winded. Cooper sat staring blankly at him. It was then that the others realised Cooper knew what was wrong and was protecting Jones with his silence.

'That half-track seems nearer,' said Harding. No one replied. Then Reilly said: 'Not aircraft engines anyhow. The Luftwaffe is taking so long to get here I've been wondering if our boys shot all the buggers down. Strange to think none of our aircrews have any idea they're doing us a favour. They don't even know we exist.'

'We'll thank 'em if we get the chance,' growled Hurst, getting to his feet. 'Come on, lads. That's enough rest and chat. Let's be having you.' He had them, still had them in spite of almost twenty-four hours of continuous marching over very rough country. That fantastic period of training was showing some dividends — for four of them.

Hurst reached the rock fall first and waited for them there. As they trudged towards him they could see the angry lines etched into his face.

'What's up?' asked Reilly.

'That's what's up. We are having a lucky day, aren't we?' He pointed down the hill at a newly cleared ride through the forest beneath them. 'Just wide enough for a half-track to get up, I shouldn't wonder, and we can't be very far ahead of them now. It's not on the maps of course, just another little surprise — like you!' He had added spitefully, as

Jones arrived. Again Jones said nothing, just looked sullenly at Hurst; the same response he had given to every curse and question directed at him in the last three hours.

'Well,' said Hurst, 'we now have to get across this mucky bit of country before Jerry arrives, whether he comes by land or air. Get moving as quick as you can but watch your step. A broken ankle gets you a bullet. First one across covers the rest. Now move! Move!'

The mass of boulders rose fifty feet above them. The white stones glared fiercely, made them cringe, yet demanded a constant, wide-eyed scrutiny if they were to avoid breaking a limb or falling heavily. They shrugged their weapons and rucksacks into yet another uncomfortable position and started to climb. Below them the half-track crept slowly up the valley side, it was still out of sight but the engine sounded louder.

Hurst and Reilly took the lead, followed by Cooper, with Jones and Harding at the rear. Harding, struggling to adjust his pack, started last, just behind

Jones. He watched Jones fumbling for footholds and saw him bring both hands into play to drag himself up on to the rocks. As he did so, his right hand, the one he had been holding against his body, left a reddish-brown print on the side of a boulder. Harding stared at the palm print: the good luck talisman of the desert cities perfectly defined on a rock splintered from its neighbours by the severity of an Arctic winter! He now knew what Cooper knew but did not understand how Jones had been hurt; the most obvious explanation simply did not occur to him. All he could think about was that here was the seed of yet another tragedy. He climbed ahead and away from Jones as fast as he could.

The rock fall was about four hundred yards wide at that point; a frozen sea of harsh, irregular, leg-snapping pits and spikes, in which the strain on ankles was matched by the strain on the eyes. Ironically, it was now that the cumulus clouds began to grow very rapidly with the up-welling heat of high summer. The effect was to dapple the confused surface of the rock fall with many patches of moving, varying light and shade. This effect further confused them and their decline into light-headedness worsened with every jarring step. They all took more than twenty minutes to cover those four hundred yards.

At the far side of the rocks they had to negotiate a vicious, unstable slope of wobbling, rickety boulders that led down to clear, firm ground. Here, with weapons ready, Hurst and Reilly waited for the others. They watched Cooper and then Harding move tiredly and shakily past them. 'They're still O.K.,' murmured Reilly. 'But what the hell's happening to Jones?' Hurst shook his head. They waited a long time.

Jones stood before them, outlined black against the sun. He began to edge his way towards them. In the instant before his ankle turned all the watchers knew he would fall, but none of them was prepared for the huge quantity of boulders and dust he brought down with him. They threw themselves to one side as Jones plunged helplessly down the slope.

The noise was appalling as great boulders clashed together and smaller stones skidded across the slope like bullets. Jones vanished.

As the dust dispersed and the last stones rolled to a halt, the four dust-caked survivors began their grim search. They found him at the bottom of the slope; his head and chest were free but his lower trunk and legs were buried under several tons of rock. They stood round the half-buried, dust-smothered body, coughing and retching. 'Christ! We'll never get him out from under that lot,' someone whispered.

'I don't think we'll have to,' said Hurst, crouching over the body. He stepped back so they could all see that Jones's neck was broken. His eyes were closed, his face relaxed and unmarked except for the film of dust sticking to the skin. Cooper bent over him, then looked despairingly at Hurst. 'But he's not dead.'

Slowly, Hurst slipped off the safety catch that had been a protection against shooting himself had he fallen on the rocks. He knew what he had to do.

'Noise?' queried Reilly, half-drawing his knife.

'He's made enough already,' said Hurst, stepping forward.

'No,' said Cooper, flatly. 'Not like that.' He turned back to Jones, leant down, put his hands on Jones' head and pulled hard. 'It's all right now, Major. Someone else can sort 'is pack.' He turned his back on them, walked away and sat on a rock. White-faced, he watched Reilly and Hurst wrench the pack from the body. The carefully packed explosives, ammunition and iron rations were removed, but the more innocuous items that a partisan might be expected to carry were left in the rucksack. They could not find his gun. It was buried with his legs.

Harding took no part in this hasty searching and sorting. He was too busy fighting for self-control. The numbness of mind that had protected him since Anders died had been stripped away by the ferocious single-mindedness of his companions. He felt as if all his vital nerves had been severed by a single razor stroke; reality was so very much more hideous than his craziest imaginings.

This was the second killing in a few hours and neither of the victims had been killed by the enemy. Was it possible Hurst had turned traitor and was wrecking the operation before it really got under way? Stupid idea. But he would have said it was just as stupid to imagine Hurst killing Anders, Cooper killing Jones; yet these things had happened. The heat, the glare, the dust, his fearful, uncontrollable mind combined to make him horribly dizzy. He was on the point of vomiting when Reilly snapped his fingers at him.

'Wake up soldier! Get this in your pack!' He thrust a bundle into his arms. Later, Harding was to wonder if he had done as he was told; he had no recollection of doing so.

Hurst walked across to Cooper. 'Put this gear in your pack and we'll be off.' Cooper took the equipment from him without speaking. Hurst made no attempt to help him adjust his pack but stood watching him closely. 'I'm sorry, Andy.'

'Not your fault, Major. He always said we was too lucky. Today our luck ran out.'

'What went wrong with him before he fell?'

'E'd been shot.'

'*What?*' Hurst's astonishment was shared by the others.

'Yes. He was shot in the fight this morning.'

'Bloody Hell! I knew Jerry got off a few rounds but had no idea anyone was hit.'

'As you said earlier, Major — with our luck today . . . '

'But why didn't you . . . ?'

'Tell on him? Is that your question when you bloody well knows the answer? No prisoners, no wounded you said. He wanted to last out long enough to be useful. I think he might've asked to stay 'ere and hold up anyone follering us.'

'Oh, Christ!' groaned Hurst. 'He knew better than that and so did you. We can't afford any fucking nonsense like that! Mock heroics by our brave wounded! We couldn't be sure he'd die so we couldn't leave him. He might have been captured and that would have been the end for all of us. Why the hell did you wait 'til now to finish him off? All you've done is waste a lot of time when we can least afford it. Now we're doing the same thing standing here and arguing. Get up that bloody hill as quick as you can. Come on! Move!'

With the precise timing of that fate-managed day the roar of the half-track came ripping over the rocks at them as it burst out of the trees on the far side of the rock fall. They all looked at Hurst, saw rage swept from his face by the need to make the right decisions instantly.

He sent Reilly down the hill with orders to cut back over the rocks and knock out the half-track and crew when he heard the rest of his own party open fire. Then Hurst led the other two away from the rocks, through a grove of stunted trees and up the first part of the valley wall. As soon as they were high enough to look back over the trees and down on to the rocks they spread out ten yards apart and concealed themselves among some boulders. They removed their packs, checked their weapons and settled down to wait. Hurst's last softly spoken order drifted across the hillside,

'Get every one of them.'

They had a long wait, the longest rest of the day. The silence became oppressive; a heavy draped backcloth against which the sounds of the last hour were played back in their minds: engine roar, stumbling footsteps, dull thumping of tumbling boulders, soft snap of safety catch. Jones was dead; a very different matter to the death of their guide. One of their own team dead. This was personal loss, breaking the thin make-believe veneer of their own invincibility. Who would be next? And when? Now?

Poor old Jones, thought Harding, guiltily. He'd never liked him, never made any real contact. Any feelings resembling sorrow were self-pity. He could not adjust quickly enough to this tide of disasters; he even doubted his own sanity in the face of his companions' absolute single-mindedness.

These feelings of inadequacy and unreality were reinforced now he had time to look round at the dark, majestic land to which they had come. The massive scale of the heights and depths, the great sweeps of bare rock and of green-black forests all pointed his own minuteness and insignificance. Yet it was his life that was threatened; the passive, claustrophobic hills merely aroused the stupid resentful questioning he had tried to suppress: Why me? Why me?

He looked round from their position. They were right against the valley wall that led up to the plateau. Their only retreat was a steeply climbing trackway behind them; they would never make it under the guns of their pursuers; they would be picked off in the first hundred feet. Once more they had to annihilate the opposition, cut them down and butcher the wounded. He wiped the sweat off his hands and turned back to the view ahead. Below him the rock fall was spread out like a bridal veil; decorated with silver threads when the sun shone, soiled and discoloured in the shade. No sign of them yet. No sign of Jones's body either; the spot where he had died was hidden from their position by the tops of the trees. Only slow drifting dust betrayed his fall and their retreat; dust that would beckon on the hunters until they were cut down. No sign yet.

A movement above his head caught his eye. He looked up, frightened that somehow they were to be attacked from above. A large cloud dragged gently along the plateau edge; nothing else moved. He shivered, sweat congealing on his face; he was cold now the sun was hidden but dared not replace his anorak in case the movements betrayed them. In one way the clouds were a blessing; perhaps they would be spared an attack from the air. If they could fight off the men following them they might get clean away. He did not believe this would happen; chance, ill-luck and stupidity had combined to trap them. This would be a last stand. He knew it, but did the others? Harding glanced sideways at his companions; their faces were expressionless as they stared ahead. Then Hurst looked in his direction and smiled at him.

He knows, thought Harding. He knows what I'm thinking. He knows these feelings: terrible burning sensations in finger tips, face and skin; the hollowness of one's body, the wracking cramps of fear; the feeling that bladder and limbs are beyond control. He knows the feelings and the thoughts. He knows enough to get us out. He must do. He must. If anyone can get us out, he can. He can. A feeling of calmness, of resignation began to permeate his mind and body. He stared along the deep, dark groove of the valley.

A head showed briefly on the far rim of the rocks, then disappeared. There was a sudden, scuffling rush and three grey figures came up on to the rocks and crouched behind some large boulders. Other figures appeared and also went to ground. There was a long pause and then the first group of Germans rose and came forward about twenty yards. The operation was entirely correct and meticulously executed; as one group moved the other group covered them. There were ten soldiers, well trained, well disciplined, and they were all to die; to die because they had not followed their quarry by a direct route. If they had stood among their dead comrades on the *saeter* they would not now have moved into the white rocks, but waited for reinforcements before making contact. But they were tragically ignorant, believing they were pursuing a ragged, ill-equipped band of partisans.

Hurst waited until the Germans at the rear were moving forward and silhouetted against the rocks. His first shots brought them down, then all three machine-guns, perfectly positioned ahead of the advancing hunters, chopped up the remnants of the patrol. The survivors went to ground among the rocks but found no protection from an enemy looking down on them; bullets still split open heads and ploughed into backs. The roar of the guns once more echoed wildly round the valley as Reilly mopped up the crew of the half-track on the far side of the rocks. Then came the flat crack of a grenade as he blew up the powerful engine. Then, as at dawn, the silence of the mountains closed in.

Harding lay still and stared across the valley. It had been easier than at Dunkirk; they had been too far away for him to see their faces. Something irritated the stubble on his chin and he rubbed his hand over his jaw, looked at his palm and saw blood. He had bitten through his lip. He looked round furtively. Hurst was watching him. They grinned feebly at each other. At least he fired this time, thought Hurst.

No one moved for about five minutes then Hurst walked swiftly across to Harding. 'You stay and cover us. Cooper will come with me.'

They raced down the hill and vanished into the grove of trees. Nothing moved in the rocks. Harding watched and waited, saw his men move obliquely on to the rock fall leaving him a clear field of fire, saw a German raise his gun but did not have to fire. Reilly shot him in the back from his position on the far side of the rocks.

The Sergeant joined the other two and together they searched for survivors. There was one weeping, wounded boy to shoot, then they climbed down from the rocks for the last time. They rejoined Harding, put on their packs and began the climb back to the cloud-strewn plateau they had left only a few hours ago.

10

They walk together through the bright morning. He had found her in the cool meadow below the black hills and now leads her back to the village. He is remote from her somehow, feels himself to be adrift in his own terrible weariness. Light-headed with exhaustion, experiencing a physical weightlessness after removing his heavy pack, his feet not feeling the road, he drifts beside her. He is invisible, indifferent, detached. When she turns towards him, smiling sadly, he looks at her dumbly. She is Nina, the Dutch girl in her blue dress, yet she is the wife of Anders Rogstad. Grief and fear, bewilderment and lassitude, condemn him to silence.

They enter the tiny village. The narrow street is lined with women and children standing silent. Behind them, in the cottage windows and on the roofs, are the vile, grey figures; guns point into the little crowd. Somewhere a house burns; smoke drifts across the street. They walk between the walls of white faces, their feet falling soundlessly on the road. Without knowing why, he drops back and walks behind her. He wonders who has betrayed her. Then she turns her head and looks at him. He it was who brought her from the meadow. Harding can offer no defence against her gaze, only bow his head in weariness.

In the road before them lies a body shrouded in grey canvas. Standing facing them across the body is a short, dark man in officer's uniform. He waits for them to reach him, gives that ridiculous salute and speaks. The woman answers but Harding is silent. But he knows, without understanding how he knows, that this is Stampf. It is sufficient to know. Words add nothing.

The woman stands over the covered corpse. Stampf pulls back the sheet and she crouches beside the body, screening it from Harding. He tries to step forward, to see that poor face once more, perhaps to close the eyes this time, but his feet do not respond.

A child is led out from a doorway. Its bruised, contorted face becomes more distorted at the sight of the mother. They cling to each other before the silent crowd. Stampf explains that the woman must betray the partisans or lose the child. Silence. Orders are given. The child is dragged from its mother by two pale-faced guards. Harding stands immovable, shackled by the same despair and incomprehension he had felt when Anders was shot. The mother begins to plead, falling on her knees before Stampf. She swears she can tell him nothing because she knows nothing. Her desperate pleas are so obviously rooted in truth that Stampf hesitates. Then he gives the signal. There is gunfire from behind the church, echoes of shots rebound from the houses, the woman falls beside the body.

Another child, chosen at random, dragged from its sobbing mother. The questions are asked again but the woman cannot answer. There is a new sound — the murmur of the crowd. It is aimed at the mother as much as at the murderers. Then a return to silence as the grey men raise their rifles. The woman struggles to her feet to plead again and Harding sees the face of the corpse for the first time. It is Jones.

Harding cannot hear his own laughter but feels himself shaken by it. All faces turn to him. Murmured protests, Stampf's commands, echoing gunfire, his own laughter, are all mingled. He is rooted to the spot but they cannot reach him. The woman throws herself towards him, begs him to speak. But the laughter and gunfire gushing from his mouth continue to sound round the village. He can save them with words if he speaks but he can only laugh and shoot them. The laughter reaches him now, it is deafening, deadly, never-ending. That silly woman — like a yo-yo. He begins to shriek hysterically, tears of laughter roll down his cheeks.

In a last agonised appeal Nina throws herself forward again. This time the barriers go and she reaches him, touches him, covers his gaping, laughing, shouting mouth. Shakes him, shakes him, covers his face with her hands. Her voice reaches him for the first time: 'Please, for God's sake stop! Stop!' A hand claws at his shoulder, shaking him, shakes him. 'Stop it! Stop it!'

A great roar from the crowd, roaring for his death. A roaring in his ears. He struggles to turn his head, to twist himself clear of the hands that blanket his face. He is lying on his back, threshing with his arms, trying to free nose and mouth from an iron grip. He begins to float away into darkness as the pain in his chest increases. In darkness above him floats the face of Cooper. It floats back and forth over his head. Then he is free, alive and free, chest heaving, gulping great draughts of cold air.

Cooper sat back on his heels, pointing his torch at the ground. 'Christ! When *you* dream you really dream, don'cher?' Harding stared up into his frightened face, thinking even that dream was no worse than reality.

'Sorry,' he mumbled. 'Sorry. Didn't know. But where's the Major? What's happened?'

'It's all right. Calm down, mate. 'E's on sentry go outside.'

'No, I'm here,' growled Hurst, sticking

his head into the tent. 'I thought I'd better check you hadn't throttled the noisy bugger.' He glared at Harding. 'Are you O.K. now? Finished dreaming?'

'Yes. Yes, I think so.' He was still breathing hard. 'I'm sorry, sorry about the noise. I — I didn't know.' There was an awkward pause. There was no sound other than the hiss of rain and its irregular drumming on the ground-sheets that formed their crude tent.

Harding became aware of the thick, fetid atmosphere: odours of sweat, stale food, damp clothing mingled with sharper smells of paraffin and oiled metal. He looked sullenly at his guardians, squatting like trolls beside his sleeping bag their worried faces glowing evilly in the pale, yellow torchlight. He wondered what it was he had cried out but dared not ask. The silence and the oppressive, familiar mustiness of the tent hung about them like sour incense. He cast round for something to say.

'Heard anything of Reilly?'

'Yes,' said Hurst. 'There was an explosion some miles east of here about an hour ago. Joe's doing his best to convince Jerry we've escaped into Sweden.' They fell silent again. Cooper shrugged himself back into his sleeping bag and then switched off the torch. Hurst muttered something about fresh air and abruptly left the tent; he preferred the silence of sentry duty to the dumb misery of his men.

Harding could not go back to sleep. His restless, taut mind led him again through the hard grind of the cross-country march from the rock fall. That terrible climb out of the valley had really torn him apart. Then, as the climbing became easier, driving rain had lashed them. No one had complained; the weather had saved them from the Luftwaffe. Their race across the plateau had been to a nagging accompaniment of aircraft droning low over their heads as the enemy groped for them through the blanket of cloud. At last, the search was called off and they were once more alone in the huge silence of Norway.

Harding's confused thoughts pressed in on him now as they had in the submarine. The dreary days of waiting in that steel casket had germinated too

166

many dark thoughts before the operation began. But he did not want to think about the submarine — cramped, frightening, smelly — so much like the tent. He did not want to think about Jones. He did not want to return to his dreams.

He was disgusted that he could not control his wandering mind. Was it simply that he had only just identified the real test: when it matters can you cut off all feeling and all imagination? Hurst and Reilly knew what they were talking about when they said that no amount of training could prepare a man for all the pressures of action. Hurst would certainly be in control of *his* thoughts as he crouched in the rain.

But Hurst, although not so self-centred, was equally troubled in his mind. He was bitterly aware of the costs so far incurred: a third of his party lost, morale badly damaged and the enemy fully alerted. The efficiency with which his team had wiped out two enemy units in the same day must have betrayed them. The local Commandant would realise he was dealing with something far more deadly than a group of ill-equipped, underfed partisans.

He wondered if his team was still an efficient unit. Cooper was certainly rattled by Jones's death. He had never worked out the relationship there; they were certainly not queer. Perhaps hatred of Jerry was their common bond; he just did not know. One thing he did know was that Harding was behaving like a pregnant schoolgirl, and they hadn't even arrived at the target.

Everything depended on Joe. If he could lay a good trail at the frontier Jerry might just swallow the bait. Even if the enemy remained alert he might cut back patrols and air searches. But Joe had to get back; the job was off if he bought it. 'Watch it, Joe. For Christ's sake watch it!'

Hurst shook his head disbelievingly: he had spoken aloud. Savagely cursing himself, he pulled his cape closer, pressed himself hard down among the rocks. All he needed now was himself as talkative sentry! But he could not stop worrying about Joe Reilly, even though he was confident of his ability to deal with any sort of trouble.

Joe was not in trouble but was busy getting others into fatal trouble. He was crouched down only twenty yards from a German guard post at the frontier. He had listened to the two sentries discussing the radio messages about an enemy group to the west, had heard their complaints about the filthy weather, and had heard the fat, stupid Corporal suggest fetching two mugs of coffee. Reilly was waiting impatiently for him to do just that. He was tired of pretending he was a boulder, he was soaking wet and, most important of all, he had cut a hole in the frontier wire an hour ago and did not want it discovered before he was ready. He had also sneaked through the wire, crossed the open ground, and buried a charge under the Swedish wire. He was not so concerned about that because his charge was well hidden. He was more worried that the Germans might start patrolling their side of the frontier. He did not know the German commander had cancelled all patrols until reinforcements arrived at dawn. Stampf could not risk a third disaster, nor did he believe it possible for the enemy force to reach the frontier area before midday tomorrow.

The Corporal went into the hut and Reilly had his knife in the other man's back before the door was shut. He lowered the body to the ground, placed his explosives against the side of the hut and slipped back into the rocks.

The Corporal came out of the hut with two mugs of coffee, shouting a coarse remark at his more fortunate comrades sitting round the red hot stove. He shut the door with his foot, cursing as some hot coffee splashed onto his wrist. He walked round to the side of the hut and tripped over the body. He shouted angrily as the coffee mugs smashed against the hut. Then he realised what he had trodden on. He just had time to feel the terrible knot of fear cramping his stomach before Reilly set off the charge. The explosion, splintering wood, screams of agony and fear, random shooting, the crackling roar of fire as the shattered stove ignited the wreckage, bewildering contradictory commands, all brought a smile to Reilly's face as he moved away towards the wire.

He waited five minutes and then pulled the charge under the Swedish wire. It was unfortunate that by then several Swedish soldiers had arrived and were crouching near the mine.

As Reilly moved silently away towards the north-west he knew he had laid a good trail: desperate party blows up German post, cuts wire, crosses no man's land, blows up the Swedish wire and then escapes into Sweden leaving dead and dying on both sides of the frontier.

★ ★ ★

Their luck with the weather continued. The next day was one of low, protective clouds and heavy rain, and they moved steadily across country all day and the next night. They were very tired and needed the long rest periods which Hurst allowed. Nevertheless, they made good progress towards the second, more distant of the two rendezvous points arranged with Reilly. Had the day been fine they would have had to lie low until evening and met him at the nearer point. The bad weather enabled them to push on a further twenty miles.

The meeting with Reilly was a triumph. Harding and Cooper fell on his neck. They slapped his back, shook his hand and insisted on carrying his pack and machine-gun for him. They were ridiculously happy to see him again. Their depression, which had deepened with every rain-soaked mile, was immediately lifted; they were almost light-headed with relief. Everything was fine now Joe was back and had laid a false trail. Hurst was secretly delighted with their reactions. and unnerved by his own. He could only stare at Joe's exhausted face and mumble something about him being a bloody long time. But Joe understood what he meant.

When they had all calmed down a little, Hurst drew Reilly to one side.

'How did it go?'

'Fine, Major. No snags. Tell you about it later.'

'How long do you need, Joe?'

'Gimme couple hours and hot meal. I'll be O.K.'

'Sure?' said Hurst, looking into the white face, the sunken eyes. 'I think the weather will hold for the rest of the day, so you can have longer if you like. You must have been moving pretty fast the last few hours.'

'Can't be sure about weather. Know how quickly it changes here. Anyway, I'll be better off moving and warm than sheltering and cold. Must get to Lion tonight.'

'Right, Joe. Don't worry about it. Have a drink from the flask and get your head down. We'll see to the food, we'll fill all the water bottles and set up the radio.'

'You'll send message today — now?'

'Yes, Joe. Don't worry. Get some sleep.'

Reilly crawled into the makeshift tent Cooper and Harding were erecting. He could not wait for them to finish the job, he had to lay down at once or die. Harding crawled in beside him and asked how things had gone. Reilly looked at him unbelievingly, opened his mouth to swear at him, then closed it again. He made one, last tremendous effort to be civil: 'Not now, sonny, later,' he mumbled and passed out.

When Reilly was shaken awake four hours later he found himself in the familiar world of damp and cramp, of cooking and stove fumes. But it was a strange new world as well. Their shelter was now dominated by the gleaming bulk of the radio.

It had a deeper significance than was suggested just by its size and weight: it was a means of changing their world completely. Once they sent the coded signal they would have five days to complete the operation. On days three and four a specially selected strike force from Bomber Command would start out each night for the Norwegian coast. If Hurst did not call them in they would bomb alternative targets in the south; if they were called in they would bomb the research station. But on the fifth night they would attack the research centre irrespective of any messages received. They would attack even if they knew Hurst's party was inside the station.

They were about to plunge into time future, into day one, day two, into third day or fourth day since the message was sent. They would leave forever the world of days past since landing, days lost, days since Anders died, days since Jones died.

In the early evening they cut the knot which tied them to the past. Three hours after sending the signal and hearing the curt acknowledgement, they climbed down the steep slope above the Lion Head. The low cloud and fine drizzle had reduced visibility to five yards so there was no chance they would be seen; equally, there was no hope of seeing their target on the far side of the valley.

At the bottom of the slope they shuffled cautiously along the narrow ledge that led to the cave. They edged their way between the rock face on one side and the bottomless mist-filled pit on the other. Vertigo threatened them as the movement of cloud and rain changed their ledge into a narrow, swaying rope that unrolled itself endlessly out of the fog. Suddenly, the reassuring roughness of the rock wall was no longer brushing their left shoulders. They had reached the cave. The mouth of the Lion Head closed on them.

PART THREE

The Kill

11

Dawn. The heralds were pale vermilion brush strokes across the pale blue-greys of cloud-feathered sky; forerunners of a day already spilling over Karelia. Against the pastel weave of sky the cold, silent land stood up blackly; the Nordic land ruled by the most savage of men's gods. At dawn, Norway is a harsh, bitter land unable to escape its legacies of mystery and terror.

The evil moment passed when the highest slopes were flooded by a luminiferous light. Above the calm, slate-grey seas of the high plateaux floated the cluster of pink-tinted peaks which mark the link with Sweden. Then, almost imperceptibly, the pink tints of dawn were overwhelmed by the clear, pale yellows of morning. As the globe turned east the mountains swung under the sun and light speared between the peaks and struck the lower slopes; sinister form and shadow were revealed as no more than faces of ice-scoured rock.

All rocks, all trees facing east glowed with the warming sun. Only in the fiord depths and on the west facing walls did the great stain of night remain. Here was a world that never knew the true daybreak, that never felt the fresh touch of early morning. Here the change came late and with swift brutality; black night was destroyed in an instant as the full light of day was suddenly poured down into the dark pit.

The Lion Head was in light while the east end of the fiord was still black with clinging night. The watcher lying on the ledge outside the cave was careful not to move abruptly; he knew that in spite of his insignificance in that enormous landscape a sudden movement might betray him. He was held up to view in the bright dawn while his adversaries still skulked watchfully in the darkness below.

Hurst was joined by Harding. Huddled together for warmth they lay staring down into the black cauldron which was blocked off from the sun by its rim of high ground to the east. Slowly, the view emerged from the shadows. Below them on their own shore was revealed the outline of the dormitory block perched on a narrow rib of rock that stretched out into the water. From this headland a small pier pointed accusingly across the fiord to the patch of night still slinking at the base of the hills. There, in light reflected from their own valley-side, they saw the features of their model suddenly take on the shapes of reality: the delta flat supporting the main buildings, the temporary huts which had been added, the linking strips of tarmac, the parade square, the sports field; all clearly revealed as the shadow edge retreated.

Then, inverted, the perfect mirror reflection began to grow on the black glass sheet of the fiord. The weird lighting of the scene, the polished obsidian water and patterns of creeping darkness and light combined to distort all sense of distance. The watchers knew they had only to extend their arms to pick up those tiny buildings or fracture the reflection with their finger tips.

The last trace of night was swept aside and they became aware of the dam soaring above the camp. It leapt out of the darkness, higher and bigger than they had imagined it. They stared at it apprehensively; even the revelation of the very small turbine house below it and attached to it by short umbilical pipes did not correct the impression it was a very big dam. With the bright sky behind it, and the rock wall on which it stood still in shadow, it appeared to tower above them as well as above the camp. Hurst cautiously raised his glasses for a closer view.

'Oh, God.' He whispered. So deeply felt, so agonised was the exclamation that for a terrible instant Harding thought the Major had been hit by a sniper.

'What is it? What is it, Major?'

'Look at the dam. Here — use the glasses, never mind about the light, just don't move them quickly.'

Harding peered through the hooded binoculars, as always finding himself bewildered by a view so enlarged he was swallowed up in it. With some difficulty he focused on the dam. The two guards sprang at him through the lenses; they appeared so close he flattened himself hard against the rock ledge. They were walking slowly towards each other along the top of the dam, hugging themselves in the sharp coldness of the dawn.

'Guards,' he said, stupidly.

'Look at the north end of the dam.'

'Hell! There's a hut, a large, new wooden hut. A guard house?' He lowered the glasses slowly and looked helplessly at Hurst. The Major's twisted smile was not reassuring.

'Well, John. What do you make of it then? How new is the guard house? Does this mean they expect us or does it mean that they decided to guard the dam anyway? Is that hut two days or two weeks or two months old?'

'How can one tell, Major? It's new, even from here one can see it's new. But we cannot deduce anything from that.'

'Too bloody right! The only certainty is it'll get in our way when we blow the penstock. Now we're a man short we've found we need him more than ever. No, don't use the glasses again. We'll have to save them for the afternoon when the sun's behind us. I'm not giving our position away at the last moment. Anyway, once it's full light we'll get a pretty good view without glasses.'

Reilly and Cooper crawled out of the cave and across the ledge. Harding wondered if they had sensed the crisis even when asleep.

'What's up?' said Reilly, thickly.

'A guard hut on the dam is what's up — and recently up too,' explained Harding.

'For our benefit, you reckon?' asked Reilly, suddenly wide awake.

'Can't say,' replied Hurst. 'It's new but we can't tell how new. No, don't use the glasses now, we're in full light up here.'

Harding stared ahead knowing that using the binoculars all afternoon would be no help to him. He could deduce no more from seeing the real thing than he could from looking at the model in England. A feeling of disquiet possessed him; perhaps he was disappointed that the camp did look so much like the model. Had he expected some startling alterations to have occurred so that he could instantly identify what was going on?

'Well, Captain?' said Hurst.

'I don't know,' said Harding, feebly. There was a long silence while they all looked at him with something akin to suspicion; they had been conditioned to expect him to know everything about the camp, to give them a lead at this point. Hurst was the only one to accept his answer at face value. Harding shrugged his shoulders. 'I don't know. We have got to go down there.'

'Thank you,' said Reilly, sourly.

'We can't avoid dealing with the guards either,' said Hurst. 'But we'll work that one out with all the other problems later today.'

'Right, I'll get breakfast,' said Cooper, apparently quite unconcerned, even though he knew the guards on the dam would be dealt with by the men who blew the dam. He and Hurst were the top explosives experts in the team.

'Wait,' said Hurst.

Clearly and distinctly through the still air and across calm water came the sounds of military activity: hoarse commands, stamp of feet, rattle of arms.

'But we're miles away,' someone said.

'Now you know how sound carries over water,' said Hurst. 'You couldn't have a clearer warning, could you? We may be far away and high above the camp but sound travels in strange ways in these hills. So keep things quiet. And no cooking until we've had another look at our cave.'

When they had arrived the night before they had been too exhausted to explore the cave very thoroughly. They now discovered that the outer cave ran back into the hillside, narrowed to a mere passageway and then widened again to form a second chamber. Cooper set up his stove in this inner cave and began to prepare a meal.

The outer cave was large enough for them to lay out all their equipment without disturbing their sleeping area, while the ledge outside formed a pleasant, sunny veranda. Their only restriction was that of keeping noise at a low level. After the haste, the damp, the exhausting flight of the last few days their new home seemed luxurious. They could rest, eat, check equipment or doze in the sun without fear of discovery. They could even relieve themselves at leisure in the depths of the inner cave; no more crouching behind rain-soaked rocks while irritable colleagues urged you to hurry. They were saved from the guerrilla's constant fear of being caught with his pants down. It was not surprising that breakfast was a festive meal in spite of the awful food. Reilly's laconic account of his adventures at the frontier also cheered them up. Confidence and optimism returned; the certainties of failure and death were temporarily pushed aside.

They spent the rest of the morning checking all their equipment. Each rucksack was completely unpacked and all the contents examined in detail. Cooper's rucksack and pockets disgorged the radio, three hundred feet of rope, a pair of binoculars, a torch, ammunition, iron rations (from Jones's rucksack), a small flask, spare socks, spare watch and spare parts for the stove.

Hurst's rucksack, and its modified pockets, contained a two-man rubber dinghy packed in a rubber container sixteen inches by twelve inches by twelve inches. This German commando equipment excited their admiration more than anything else they possessed. Hurst had also been carrying detonators, wire, binoculars, iron rations, ammunition, spare torch, radio spares, and spare socks. The total weight of his load was an index of his great strength and made Reilly and Harding a little embarrassed about unpacking their own smaller loads.

Reilly conjured up a one-man dinghy, five hundred feet of rope, explosives, fire bombs, binoculars, first-aid kit, a small tin of fluorescent paint, a small paint brush and, inevitably, spare socks. Harding added more rope, more ammunition, more explosive, more food and a miscellany of odd items including Hurst's vacuum flask, plates, lavatory paper, Very pistol, wire cutters and air pump.

When all this was laid out beside their

sleeping bags and weapons it seemed incredible that they had been able to carry so much. But, as Cooper ruefully pointed out, the only really heavy item was the radio he had carried; most of the other equipment was fairly light. The other obvious point was that the loss of Jones's rucksack had not reduced their stores to below the safety level.

Their only deficiencies were food and water, and both of these could be made good when they moved out to the fiord and to the hidden stores on the hills. They had filled their water bottles before climbing down to the cave and could expect this to last them for at least another two days. The snags were that a lot of water was needed to reconstitute their rations, and also that the men were nearly as dehydrated as their food. But in spite of this they were all cheered by the great mound of equipment at their feet.

'Well,' said Hurst, 'it's not Christmas yet, so let's get working. Only two things matter this morning: checking every bit of gear, and getting some more rest. This afternoon we'll start continuous watch on Jerry.'

They checked every weapon, every magazine, every container. The dinghies they left alone since their cases were completely undamaged; the problem of repacking them was too awe-inspiring to consider. When they had checked all the equipment Hurst made them check their clothing. He personally inspected each man's boots, paying particular attention to soles and laces. Then he made them check every button they were wearing; any that had been wrenched loose had to be restitched, as did any tears in their clothing.

Reilly produced a German 'housewife' or 'frau' as he called it and set up shop in one corner of the cave. 'Even this little 'frau' is better than our stuff,' he growled. 'As for that radio, it's a miracle. We've unpacked it twice and each time the bleeder's worked straight off. Can you imagine that happening with a British set? Just as well we do have to use Jerry gear, if you ask me. If we want to win the war we need to capture the hell of a lot of

Jerry gear first. The only thing I miss is me Bren.'

'We're all right though, Joe,' said Hurst, rather annoyed at this defeatist talk.

'Blimey, Major, I'll say we are. Best men and best gear.' The indignation in his voice brought smiles to all their faces. Where would they be without Joe?

They ate again at midday and then Harding and Cooper were told to rest on their beds. Hurst and Reilly lay on the ledge outside the cave and examined the target through binoculars. They could not be observed because the ledge sloped upwards and away from the cave mouth. They could only be seen from the air and the noise of an aircraft approaching would give them plenty of warning. For half an hour they did not speak but enjoyed the hot sun on their backs while scrutinising every part of the camp. At last, they lowered their glasses and looked at each other.

'Well, Joe?'

'Well, Major, that model they showed us was pretty good.'

Hurst smiled to himself. Joe was not

giving much away.

'Other comments, Joe?'

'No one's patrolling the fences, but that doesn't mean there are no guards at night. Can't tell from here if the fences are electrified, but even if they're not we still need the diversionary attack on the dam.'

'Do you think we can do it, Joe?'

There was a long silence.

'There's nothing in the set-up we couldn't manage, taking one thing at a time. But of course we can't do it that way; several things have got to happen at once. So I reckon we've got two main problems: timing and how to use our men. It's the second problem that worries me. At least we can take it our bright lads can tell the time once we've synchronised their watches for 'em.'

'Come off it, Joe. They're better than that even though they're bloody tired. They did pretty well when we ran into trouble. I think If we split the team so those two aren't together we'll manage all right.'

'That means you and I won't be together.'

'I'm sorry too, but that's how it's got to be. Can you really imagine Cooper and Harding breaking into the camp by themselves? For different reasons they're both pretty shaky.'

'All right then. Who gets sonny boy?'

'Sorry, Joe, you do.'

'Major, you're a rotten bugger.' They both grinned.

'I've good reasons, Joe. The crucial thing is knocking out the power supply so we must concentrate on that, and Cooper and I are supposed to be the top boys with explosives. I know you could manage it just as well but there's another factor involved: Harding gets on with you better than with me.'

'Balls!'

'He does, you know. Especially as I was the one who shot Rogstad.'

'Well, so what? I'd've done the same. Don't tell me the silly bugger believes different?'

'I'm sure he does. He thinks I'm a blood-thirsty monster. I think this is important, especially as whoever goes with him will have to kill any scientists he meets. If Jerry's doing what we think he is down there, it's quite on the cards that Harding'll meet a scientist he knew before the war. You can shoot a former pal of his and get away with it, but if I did it young Johnny would fall apart. He leans on you quite a lot, you know. For some reason he trusts you and *you* didn't kill Rogstad. I don't think you realised how much his attitude changed when we met up with you after you'd been to the frontier. He made a real effort to pull himself together then. You're effing Father Christmas, you are. Anyway, he's fed up to here with me.'

'Get away, Major. You know you like it like that.'

'All right, cheeky. Let's get down to details. How are we going to do this job?'

12

Harding and Cooper were woken by Hurst and Reilly rushing into the cave. 'Aircraft!' snapped Hurst. They listened to the sullen growl of engines grow louder and then fade away; sighs of relief from them all. 'Just a routine patrol I should think,' said Hurst. 'Well timed though, it made us wake you lads at the right time — dinner time. You've been asleep all afternoon so you can wait on us. Then it'll be your turn to keep watch.'

Harding followed Cooper to the inner cave, blearily rubbing his eyes and wondering what the other two had worked out between them while they had been lying on the ledge. They were the schemers; he and Cooper were just the cooks.

The meal was revolting but hot. They could almost feel the heat driving the last of the damp out of their bodies and through their clothes. The ersatz coffee was also unpalatable but it quenched their thirsts for a short time. 'I don't know which I like least: German mock coffee or their bog paper,' grumbled Reilly. 'As for a decent fag or a cuppa — well!'

'I thought you admired German products,' said Harding.

'Some, boy, just some.'

'Never mind, Joe, not long to go now,' said Hurst. The other two looked at him sharply. 'All right, all right, I'll tell you what we've worked out.' He lay back on his sleeping bag and looked at the roof of the cave.

'We'll go on the night of day two, tomorrow night, and attack on the night of day three. Andy and I will go for the dam, Joe and John will break into the camp. That means Joe and John will spend day three here at the cave while Andy and I'll be resting more than halfway to the dam. Details on that can wait. What is important now is to set up a continuous watch on Jerry tonight, especially for the period when we are likely to attack, say roughly 01.00 hours to 03.00 hours. As you two lucky lads have been sleeping all afternoon you'll have the early watch tonight, then Joe and I will take over later.

'We'll record everything we see that might help us: any sound, any show of lights, any special routines followed by the guards, etc. You'll be able to check on some things before dark but it's after dark that really matters; so keep your eyes skinned. If anyone comes out of that guard hut at any time for any reason I want to know. If Jerry's not expecting trouble, if Joe convinced them we're in Sweden now, they'll be careless with blackout screens over doors. Any flash of light from any point might help us. We can spend an hour together now, checking the camp layout before it gets too dark for us to see clearly. Leave the supper things for Joe and I to do later.'

They crept across the ledge and looked down on a scene which should have been familiar but was oddly transformed. The whole of the valley head was bathed in a soft, orange glow; black rocks, green trees, black water; all deeply glowing, throbbingly alive with magnificent tints of orange and orange-red of the sunset. It was a landscape depicted in the richest of stained glass; every shade and tone of orange ever imagined by man was there, repeated on myriad surfaces, myriad substances. Even the camp and the dam were given an ethereal quality by the setting sun. The view reminded Harding of childhood visits to magic lantern shows, of sitting open-mouthed, staring at the riot of colour splashing the screen and the upturned faces. He remembered the curious effect produced by sitting next to the projector and watching the magic beam sweep past him, impinging on the screen in a soundless explosion of colours. The comparison was a good one, for although the plateau above and behind them hid the sun as it slid into the western sea, they could see, could almost touch the great band of orange-red sunlight as it streaked past them along the length of the fiord and struck the mountain wall above the camp. They watched in silence.

Then, as the deep vault of the sky was

pierced with the first-seen stars, the colours in the valley began to deepen into richer reds and then into purples. Once more the view was new and fresh: distances were suddenly increased, as if the Lion Head had moved backwards out of the valley. The camp had once seemed so close they could touch it; now the red lights of evening carried it miles away, back into the mountains. The perfect reflection of the red mountains in the smooth, unruffled water elongated itself towards their own shore. For a moment the whole scene was reflection rather than reality. None of the watchers realised they were holding their breath.

The change was sudden and dramatic. A small motor launch began to move across the water towards them, carving a silver line through the mirrored scene. The ripples of the wake fragmented the reflected picture but at the same time added a moving mass of colour to the view; the water was now all wavelets, each one a silver etching on a deep red ground, every ripple flung back a flicker of fire to match the fires burning in the camp windows. No one spoke until the launch came to rest at the pier on their side of the fiord.

'Glasses,' whispered Hurst. 'Thanks. Four men on board, three get out and five get in. Bet the boat comes back again with three men in it.'

'How the hell do you get that?' asked Reilly.

'Easy,' said Hurst. 'Day shift coming off, night shift going on, but they can't leave the equipment, what ever it is, unattended, so two men stay behind. When the night shift of five arrives that'll release the two who stayed behind. They'll come across to the dormitory block with the boatman.'

'Clever Dick!' snarled Reilly, forty minutes later when the boat tied up to the pier with three men on board.

'I do my best,' said Hurst. 'The interesting thing is that if Jerry has now swopped the two shifts there's no need to use the boat later on tonight. So if we do hear it buzzing about we can assume it's being used for patrols.'

'But couldn't it be used to bring other

men to this building?' asked Harding.

'Doubt it. Jerry doesn't usually mix accommodation for servicemen and scientists. Anyway, if you listen out for the boat tonight you can check on me. The other interesting thing about that trip was that the night shift made straight for that long, low building, building J on our maps. I reckon that's your target.'

'Not only that,' said Cooper. 'Did you see what they was wearing — civvies. And one of them took his overcoat off before going indoors and 'e was wearin' a white coat.'

Harding could almost hear his companions' brains clicking. He knew it would be a waste of breath suggesting any interpretation of the facts other than the one they were so eager to accept. Those arduous weeks of conditioning left no room for doubts or hesitancy. He found himself, not for the first time, envying his companions' single-mindedness.

They continued to watch together. The splendour of the view was as much the attraction as the need to check on the enemy. They saw the fierceness of the sunset gradually mellowing to the soft purples of dusk, saw the slow spread of night back into their valley. The great stands of conifers began to merge into an indistinct army of black sentinels, only the sharply defined crowns of the tallest trees retained their individuality. Then a new element was added to the view. Pale smoke began drifting through the trees, creating the dual effects of trees burning and trees moving uphill at the same time. 'What is it?' asked Harding.

'It's all right,' said Hurst. 'It's just mist beginning to come down the hill. It's a strange effect isn't it? Makes you think the trees are going up the hill.'

Fascinated, they watched the mist patches creep down towards the water, then coalesce at the shore to form a thin blanket that slowly encroached on the dark water.

'Will it get so thick we can't see the bloody camp?' asked Cooper.

'May do,' said Reilly. 'But if you can't see the camp any more you may still be able to see the dam. So no skiving off your watch, young Andy.'

'All right, all right,' said Cooper. 'I can see why the Raf don't fancy the camp as a target.'

'It's not only the mist that worries them,' said Hurst. 'The whole set-up is a bit grim. To be absolutely safe they have to fly in at about ten thousand feet if they're to pull clear of the mountains and the frontier. From that height the camp is a pin head in size. Then don't forget the only time they can attack in daylight is at dawn; that's because they need the darkness as some protection from fighters as they come in over the North Sea. Well, you saw what happens at dawn: the target is just about the last part of the valley to come into daylight. To complete the confusion the aircrews will have the rising sun slap in their faces. No wonder they'll be grateful for some guidance from us down here. All they'll see, assuming the mist has cleared, is their own markers and they won't know if they're in the right place unless we tell 'em. That's why we can't beat it from here as soon as we get back to the cave. We have to hang on to make sure the camp is really flattened.'

'Unless it's just a holiday camp,' murmured Harding.

'Don't waste your breath and our time with wishful thinking,' snapped Hurst. 'Right, you two keep your eyes peeled from now on. Joe and I have work to do before we get our heads down. We'll clear up the cave and bring your sleeping bags out, it's getting bloody cold now. Then, when it's really dark, Joe and I'll fix up the aerial from the cave. Now don't you forget: any sound, any sight, any light and I want to know about it. Every single one. Wake us at 02.00 and we'll take over.'

It wasn't long before Cooper and Harding were settling down in their sleeping bags on the ledge while Reilly and Hurst clambered up the slope above the Lion Head pulling the flexible aerial behind them. When they had wedged it firmly in position they climbed down to the cave.

'Night, boys,' hissed Reilly.

'Good night,' said Harding, softly.

'Let's 'ope it is a good night,' said Cooper.

They did not divide up the area under

surveillance but watched the whole of the valley together. This was on Cooper's advice; he knew that if they concentrated on just half the view they were more likely to go to sleep. He had a shrewd idea that Harding was even more exhausted than he was himself.

Cooper made a full record of every sight and sound that reached them, making suggestions as to what each might be. Harding was astonished by the acuteness of Cooper's hearing; he heard laughter, doors slamming and orders given, when all Harding heard was muffled sounds drifting across the still water. He was so impressed by Cooper's efficiency he left all the recording to him. His exhaustion slowly gained control and eventually he dozed.

'See it?' hissed Cooper.

'See what?' said Harding, guiltily.

'The light on the dam.'

'I'm afraid not.'

'Christ! Don't tell me you was kipping. Bloody 'ell, it beats me why you came!'

'That'll do, Corporal,' snapped Harding, resentfully. 'Just tell me what you saw.'

'Well, dozy, I'll tell you.' Cooper's even tone suggested he was just able to control his temper. 'A light at the end of the dam. Looked like the guard hut door. Could mean the guard's changing. If that's the case there must be four men up there; two on, two off. They'd hardly march up the hill at midnight, would they?'

'No,' said Harding. 'Especially as the path up to the dam is such a long, twisting route.'

'On the other hand,' said Cooper, 'someone may be going for a piss.'

'How do we tell?' asked Harding, stupidly.

'See wot happens tomorrow night at the same time. I'll be on me way by then, but I might be in the right spot to check at this time. Mind you, mind you, we might just be perishin' unlucky and have a guard wiv very regular 'abits. But I doubt it.'

They raised their glasses again and stared out into the summer night. Although there was no moon, the star-studded sky was not black; the sun was only just below the horizon as

Norway was turned towards its next dawn. Harding felt oddly comforted by the inevitability of that dawn. Some things were reliable, fixed, immutable.

Reilly and Hurst took over from them two hours later. They came out on to the ledge while Harding was wondering if he should tell Cooper to go in and wake them. Hurst sent them back to the cave at once and said he would check their sightings in the morning. They were not sorry about that; they had spent long enough fighting off sleep.

The dawn of their second day at the cave was a dreary affair of rinsed grey clouds, with mist thick as porridge choking the lower levels of the valley. The camp and the dam had disappeared under the rising mist at about 04.00 hours, so Reilly and Hurst had little to report apart from the fact they were very cold. The four of them stood together on the ledge and looked down at the top of the mist some fifteen hundred feet below them. They felt as if they and their mountain-side were floating free of the earth below. This strange sensation, this separation from reality did not delude them; within hours they would be in the valley depths themselves. Nor did the weather mislead them into making rash forecasts; in the short time they had been in Norway they had already experienced the unpredictable nature of a changeable Scandinavian summer.

The grey morning dragged; a light drizzle began. There was little to do except re-check equipment or doze uncomfortably on top of their malodorous sleeping bags. Outside the cave, below the ledge, the mist clung obstinately to the trees on the mountain-side, obliterating all sense of space and time in a view where knowledge of space and time was their life blood.

After lunch, another poor, unsatisfying meal, the tension began to grow in them. A feeling that was compounded of fear and excitement began to rise within the core of each man. They watched each other furtively, wondering how the others were feeling, wondering how their last afternoon together would ever pass. It was something of an anticlimax to be told by Hurst that the mist was lifting, the drizzle had stopped and that they could have another look at the camp together. But out on the ledge they felt the tension revive as Hurst checked through the code lettering of the buildings in the camp. The oppressive effect of keeping their voices low added to the tension.

Hurst satisfied himself they were all letter perfect when referring to the buildings. The code letters were the same as those used on large scale maps when briefing the bomber crews. They would be used to direct bombing on to particular sections of the target. Of course, this presupposed that there would be survivors, that visibility would be good, and that at least one bomber crew was prepared to make a suicidal low level attack.

'Now for final details,' said Hurst, looking into each man's face in turn.

'Andy and I go tonight because we have a long journey to the dam. Andy's route is over the top here and I'll discuss it with him later. Joe and I go down the hill to the water. Joe will mark out the best route for himself and John to use tomorrow night. The toughest stretches will be roped, while on the flatter stretches Joe will put dabs of fluorescent paint on the trees, on the uphill side only. The route will be completely camouflaged by the trees, but we'll make sure no ropes or markers can be seen from the beach. That's a precaution in case a Jerry comes over to our side for some fishing. When we've done that I'll cross the water in the one-man dinghy, so I can approach the dam from the south side tomorrow night.

'I've given a lot of thought to the idea of going with Andy but there are real advantages in coming in from both sides. I'm not likely to be spotted crossing the water in the middle of the night, and as none of us heard anything of the motor launch last night it seems pretty certain Jerry doesn't bother with patrols. The boom at the coast and the patrols there probably seem enough to them. Well, when Joe launches me he comes back here to the cave and meets John.'

'Do I go part of the way with Cooper?' asked Harding.

'No, you do not. We can take no risks with you. You still have to be loved and cherished until you can report back by radio. In any case Andy can manage alone; it's an easy route back up to the plateau and he won't be stuck with the radio on his back this time.

'Andy and I will lay up next day and move in on the dam on night three. The same night you two go down the hill and cross to the camp in the two-man dinghy, arriving just before we blow the dam. Now, Joe and I have talked this over and, bearing in mind Andy's record of Jerry activity last night, we intend to blow the charges at 01.15 hours. As we cut off the power you two go through the wire and into building J, the one the white-coated Jerries went to. Andy and I will give all the covering fire we can including grenade attacks. We'll only be about two hundred feet above the camp so we ought to do a lot to frighten 'em. But remember, we can't get down to you in much less than an hour, unless we fall over the edge of course, so you must get yourselves out and away. We'll be operating from the north end of the dam because I'll have crossed over to help Andy deal with the guard hut.

'When you two get clear come back to the beach this side of the fiord, scuttle the dinghy and then climb back here, bringing the ropes with you. That'll help slow down pursuit — if there's anyone left in a fit state to follow you. Back here, John operates the radio, reports to the Brigadier and controls the bomber force. After that you set the charges to blow the radio and get out. Do not, repeat do not, wait for Andy and me to rejoin you here in case we're not coming back. Make for pick-up point code named 'Rosemary'. If we meet anywhere it'll be there.

'These plans are essentially the same as we discussed so often in training. All we've done is take out the part played by Jones. As a result the explosion at the dam and our covering fire will be all the diversionary activity we can lay on. We'll have to make do with that. Although I think it's enough.

'Now each of you will describe exactly what you have to do, to the rest of us. We'll go on doing this until we're word perfect and map perfect. We'll check every move together on our maps. Right, Joe, you go first. Assume you have to explain every detail to a group of dimwits.'

They spent most of that last afternoon together going through each man's plan of action; at the same time they were able to feed into their plans all their last-minute ideas and queries. Thus, it was decided to synchronise their watches and the two spare watches immediately and then check them every hour. In addition, it was agreed that Hurst, who had the toughest journey and who was also to make the first move in the attack on the dam, should take Reilly's watch as well as his own when he set out in the dinghy. Reilly would then collect a spare watch on his return to the cave. Finally, he and Harding would leave the other spare watch on top of the radio so that it was available for those of the party who got back in time to transmit the vital messages. Timing was the crux of the matter, especially with the team split and unable to contact each other except by Very pistol; a method of communication that would achieve no more than would the big bang as the penstock was blown. Harding wondered if all Hurst's persuasive arguments against carrying field radios had been misdirected; not that he could have carried a set during that mad race across country. It may have been his thoughts on this subject that caused him to voice the question which was already in all their minds.

'How long do we wait after 01.15 hours before we assume you cannot blow the dam?' The other three looked at him with something like admiration; the wording of the question was most interesting. Hurst grinned at him before he answered.

'Allow us up to half an hour, please. You will still have time to complete your part of the operation and get back here to call in the R.A.F. Of course, if you are discovered before the half-hour is up Joe will take you in straight away. Andy and I don't expect to keep you waiting; we don't want you to get a chill. I'm sure I've answered your question.

'Now we'll check through the radio procedures for when we get back here. John can run through it all first.'

13

At 19.00 hours they had their last meal together. No one doubted it was the last shared meal; too much had already gone wrong for anyone to believe otherwise. Harding had no doubts which members of the team would arrive at the pick-up point in a few days time. He knew Hurst was unstoppable and so was Reilly; they would both survive. The casualties would be Andy and himself. He thought Andy would die because he no longer cared enough. He himself was going to die through inexperience and the confusion of mind which always beset him when under pressure.

As soon as the meal was finished, Hurst and Cooper got ready to leave. Their preparations were somehow conducted in a manner which reminded Harding they were still strangers to him; even now he knew them only in the roles they had assumed in the team. He watched Hurst check his guns, his explosives, his pack; with every physical action he was coldly gearing his mind to the task ahead. Cooper was doing the same thing; the sight of him easing himself into his boots was enough to instil something like terror in the observer; his air of studied calm was rooted in thoughts of death.

The last stage of their preparations was to black up. They asked Reilly to check their blacking and not Harding. They preferred to make the most of each other's experience, and while this was only sensible, it was galling for the one man with no experience to offer. Reilly put on face camouflage as well, rubbing it into the stubble of his beard. Hurst inspected him carefully.

'You'll do, Joe.'

'Mammy,' sobbed Reilly. The silly joke did not reduce the fierce tension.

'Well, we're ready,' said Hurst, softly. 'Time for me to wish you all good luck.'

He shook Cooper's hand. 'Everything as agreed, Andy. See you tomorrow night at 01.00 hours. I'll come in at the moment that suits us best and gives us time to set the charges for 01.15. Remember: no signals. I've no doubt we'll both be ready when we should be. Good luck, Andy.'

'Same to you,' said Cooper, smiling gently up at him. 'Don't worry about me. I've got the easy journey to the dam. Best of luck, Major.'

'Well, John,' said Hurst, standing in front of him. 'We've got you here all right and I'm sure Joe'll get you into the camp tomorrow night. It will all depend on you then, but I know you can cope. Good luck, and look after that old rogue for me.' He nodded at Reilly who was weighed down under the Major's pack, and was fussing round him like a worried hen.

'Right, Joe. Here we go!'

For a moment the cave was blacked out as the two men blocked the entrance. Then they vanished over the edge of the ledge and down into the trees. There was no sound other than the rain lashing the rock face of the Lion Head.

'Me next,' said Cooper. 'It'll be really dark in an hour, then I'm off too.'

'It's a pity it's such a dirty night,' mumbled Harding. 'It's nearly as bad as that night on the plateau on the way here. Never mind, Andy, tonight is the last night marching in the rain.' As soon as he said it he wanted to cut out his tongue; he had only been talking to fill the void left by the Major's departure. Cooper was looking at him and smiling queerly.

'You don't think I'll be marchin' to the coast afterwards then? You're a cheerful Charlie!'

'I didn't mean — '

'No chum, you didn't mean it like that. That's the story of your bleeding life, that is. You're always not meaning things. You don't know how often you've missed a kick up the arse, do you? P'r'aps the Major should've let us sort you out. Never mind, you got away wiv it, your sort always do.'

'I'm sorry,' said Harding, helplessly. This was awful, terrible. He did not want them to spend their last minutes together raking over the past. But Cooper did not appear to mind.

'Why,' he said, 'I remember that

219

stuck-up expression on your face when the Major said we'd be bringin' a vacuum flask wiv us. You thought tough boys didn't need it. But you were bloody glad to get a 'ot drink when it mattered.'

'I know, I know,' said Harding. 'But I had no real experience compared with the rest of you. I was just a beginner as far as this job is concerned. Anyone else would have been just the same.' Harding almost believed he believed this himself, but Cooper just grinned at him.

'Gotta present for you,' he said, producing a small flask. 'I didn't give it to you in front of the Major in case 'e didn't like it. Some good brandy in this. Only half-full now, 'cause that Norwegian bloke had some. There's enough here for you and Joe to drink me 'ealth.' Harding stuttered his thanks, feeling even more at a loss than he did before.

'I'm gonna check me maps now,' said Cooper. 'You carry on clearing up this stinking cave before it's too dark to see wot you're doing.'

Cooper sat down at the back of the cave, switched on his torch and checked over his route. Harding clumsily cleared away the debris of the meal and rolled out his and Reilly's sleeping bags. By the time he had finished it was pitch dark.

'I'm off now then,' said Cooper, casually, as he strolled to the mouth of the cave. 'Expect I'll see you in a coupla days.'

'Good luck,' said Harding, but Cooper had gone, swinging up from the ledge to the high plateau above the cave, unworried about being seen now that night had fallen. Unlike Hurst's route which was shadowed by the mountain-side to the west and mantled by trees, his much shorter route was in full view of the camp. Harding stood on the ledge and tried to follow his progress but the darkness and the rain hid him from view.

Harding was uneasy about Cooper's abrupt departure; it worried him more than the man's rudeness. What was really wrong with Cooper? Was it grief for Jones? That was unlikely; they had hated each other. Yet it was not that simple. There was something strange there, something he could not understand now any more than when they were training together.

Harding sat in the cave alone. He had nothing to do but think or listen to the rain. He did not want to think any more, but almost at once his mind began to draw him back into the past. The cave was so much like the submarine that he began to relive that journey. From the moment they stepped aboard the atmosphere was wrong. Perhaps the crew had been reminded of the secrecy of the trip once too often and that was why they were in a sullen, uncommunicative mood. Perhaps both groups were a little too sensitive about recent losses to engage in the usual interservice back-chat. It was still the month of August and H.M.S. Eagle had been lost on the eleventh of the month. It was less than eight weeks since the capture of Tobruk and the Army was still smarting at that disgrace. Whatever the reasons, Hurst's party remained isolated from their hosts.

Harding had spent most of his time lying on his bunk trying to read the tattered, heavily thumbed books from the ship's library. On the bunks below him the other four played pontoon for hours on end. He lay and looked up at the curving roof above him: the thin skin of steel between him and the crushing weight of the North Sea. In spite of the coatings of special paints, applied so liberally that some of the rivet heads had almost disappeared, small droplets of condensation collected on them. As droplets coalesced they ran down the side of the wall and soaked into his blanket which he had carelessly thrown against the wall. Some droplets remained on the curved ceiling and grew larger, longer: stalactites growing from his own fear, his own sweat slowly stretching down towards him. The roof itself began to descend, diminishing the narrow space he occupied. The roof and his bunk began to squeeze his life from him like the giant hands of a vice. He rolled sideways, crashing from the bunk on to Cooper who was crouched below him shuffling the cards. The confusion and abuse brought him to himself. The submarine remained firm, complete.

That journey was much too closely linked with the present. He felt the cave walls throbbing with the pulse of engines. He heard the rain water dripping down outside the cave like condensation dripping from the submarine's metal skin. He burrowed deep into his bed. He slept uneasily.

He was woken by Reilly stumbling into the cave. He tried to apologise for sleeping but Reilly brushed his excuses aside, and when Harding asked how things had gone he just muttered: 'O.K.,' and would say no more. He ripped off his wet clothing and spread it out on the floor. Then he got into his sleeping bag, leaving Harding to wonder whether bad temper or worry was the reason for his curtness.

The next morning Reilly prepared breakfast before Harding woke, then served it to him in bed.

'Hope you like the service,' he said, grinning sardonically. Harding was ashamed of his own exhaustion, of being asleep when Reilly returned, of having neither food nor drink ready for him and of sleeping too long in the morning. Reilly knew what was in his mind but did not waste time on trivialities. 'How did Cooper get off?'

'All right, I think,' said Harding, not looking at him. 'But he was in rather an odd mood and left abruptly.'

'Bit shirty with you, was he?'

'It was partly that I suppose, but something else as well. He did not actually say so but I believe he does not expect to come through the raid. I don't know how much this has to do with his feelings about Jones. I don't know if it is connected with having to go in alone.'

'He's going to be with the Major so I don't see that that's the truth. It's probably Jones.'

'Yes. He appeared almost unnaturally calm to me, perhaps because he took it on himself to kill Jones. I rather expected that to lead to a certain amount of reaction afterwards,' said Harding.

'You did, did you? Fancy that! It was certainly a queer business. I suppose it was as if he wanted to keep something as

225

personal as putting Jones down within his family.'

'What do you mean by that?'

'Well, being his brother — '

'*What*?'

'All right then, his half-brother, he — '

'Wait a minute, Sergeant. This is all news to me. Were they really related?'

'Course they were: same mother, different fathers. From what I've heard it seemed a right mucky business. The mother wasn't married to either of the fathers.'

'How did you hear of this?'

'The Major told me.'

'He never mentioned it to me.'

'No reason why he should. He didn't want you too loaded down with detail, especially as you're such an imaginitive lad.'

'What do you mean by that?'

'You were dreaming again last night!'

'I can't help dreaming. I was back in the submarine.'

'God! What you need is a damned good kicking.'

'That's what Cooper seemed to think,'

said Harding, bitterly. 'You're all a great help I must say.'

'Don't start whining again! Let's face it, you haven't got the right sort of mind for this job but you've refused to accept it. Being clever, being fit, being brave are not enough. Complete control of your mind is just as vital, otherwise you go barmy with the strain. You still don't see it, do you? Not even after working with poor old Rogstad.'

'But — '

'Shut up and listen. The best man for this job is either a real tough like the Major, or a man with something missing so he doesn't feel things — a man like Jones. The snag with the first type is there aren't many of 'em, and the second type usually turn out too thick to carry out orders.

'You don't belong in either group and neither does Andy. On top of that you're too raw and he's too shaky. That's why I'd have taken over if anything happened to the Major, and why Jones was next in line after me. Then he got shot in our first action. I reckon the Major had thought he was as bullet proof as himself. That's why he was so shocked by the whole business.

'Let's face it, if you or Cooper had lagged behind he'd have sorted you out bloody quick. Somehow he couldn't face the possibility that Jones was being other than his cussed self. And you can take that expression off your face, sonny. You can't have thought you'd take charge, surely?'

'Thank you very much, Sergeant.'

'Don't be like that. We all know you can do your job, although you can't do ours. We know enough about your job to know it's far nastier than ours. Don't let the pure white lab. coats fool you. They don't fool us; we can't explode bombs until you've made 'em. Just spare us the hypocrisy. The Major only killed Anders. I'll only do the killing I have to do.'

'But — '

'All right, forget it! Let's concentrate on tonight. Tonight you do your job and I do mine. My job is to be in charge. Your job is to do as I say until we're in the lab. Then you take over.

'Just remember this: if nerves, imagination,

squeamishness, make you mess it up, my neck matters to me just as much as getting you back here to report. I can always say you were shot by Jerry. No one will be able to argue about it. And no arguments now! Just take it easy. Do what you have to do and don't try proving anything to me. I've seen it all, boy. I know you can do your job; don't fuss about mine. You're fit, you're clever, but you're too soft in the head to do what I may have to do tonight. I hope you get my meaning?'

'I think so,' whispered Harding. There were so many meanings to get! He felt strangely breathless, as though he had been running very fast. Bad temper played some part in this reaction and so did keeping abreast of this sudden, unexpected flood of words from Reilly. But most of all he was beset by fear, by fear of the coming night; fear renewed and increased by the tense, driving authority of Reilly's manner.

'Right then,' said Reilly, embarrassed by his own loquacity, 'I'll clear away if you like to get out of that sweaty bag of yours.'

Harding went out on to the ledge and looked once more across the valley. The rain had ceased, the clouds were clearing away, and the morning sun was pleasantly warm on his face. The valley was still the same in spite of the many changes of light and weather it had endured. And he was still the same person and could do nothing about it. He lay there thinking. Reilly came out and lay beside him. 'What a country,' said Harding, 'and what a view.'

Reilly grinned and nodded. 'You hardly realise it's a small country with views like this. I didn't know just how small it was myself until I had to go to the frontier the other night. Last time I was in Norway in 1940, I didn't realise how near I was to Sweden. I don't think the Major did either.'

'How did he get on last night?' asked Harding, adding waspishly; 'I've not had the chance to ask you before this.'

'All right! I don't usually jaw like that. Oh, the Major was fine in himself but had trouble getting into the dinghy. I thought the pack was heavy but it wasn't until we loaded the boat that I realised he was carrying so much more than he had originally planned. I'm afraid that in covering for Jones and Cooper he might have overloaded himself. He's working on the assumption he'll be alone at the dam and that he might not find either of the dumps on the far side of the water. The last I saw of him he had all the gear in the bottom of the boat and was lying over the top of it with his arms in the water as he paddled, and with his boots dangling across the sides like two rudders. It would have been bloody funny if only it wasn't so worrying.' He lay silent for a moment, frowning down at the fiord. 'Our route's all right anyhow. I came back up it like a dose of salts.'

'It's fortunate we don't have to carry any extra kit on our dinghy,' said Harding.

'Suppose so. These lightweight assault dinghies are all very well but I'd be happier to think you and I were setting off in a big air force dinghy. The only snag with that would be we'd all have ruptures as a result of carrying the things.'

'Where do you think the Major and Cooper are now?' said Harding.

'The Major must be up there, somewhere to the right of the dam, the south side that is. He's somewhere on the mountain-side above all that mucky scree material.'

'He covered a lot of ground last night, didn't he?'

'God, yes. He must be whacked now. Good job he's so bloody tough. I bet he's in a good position to start from tonight.

'Andy Cooper must be straight ahead from here, high up to the left of the dam. He had a good, flat run over the top and round the end of the fiord. His only real climb was down the hill towards the dam. If he's in the right place now he can see our position and the dam at the same time. Tonight, he'll only have a short walk down the hill and he'll be at the guard hut.'

14

Cooper was not in the right place. At daybreak he had turned east and climbed away from the dam. He did not know what drove him away from the sight of both the dam and the Lion Head.

He lay among some rocks and watched the pale, watery-grey sky slowly brightening after a night of heavy rain. He knew he was resting in the wrong place but was too depressed and miserable to move. His rapid progress during the night, his success in so quickly finding the supply dump had not revived his flagging spirits. Finding the dump was no real measure of his competence; any fool, even Captain Harding could have done it.

He had felt quite cheerful when he left the cave, but his relief at getting away was soon swamped by feelings of loneliness. Instead of enjoying his freedom he was disgusted to find himself disoriented by the knowledge his back was unprotected;

Jones was no longer standing at his shoulder. With every step the coldness on the back of his neck grew worse and with it grew the feeling he was being followed. He had several times stopped and waited in the darkness, straining to hear his pursuers' footsteps. On one occasion he had raced back over his tracks determined to confront his hunters. The empty hills and the sky looked down on him: a man alone, escaped from a shadow yet missing the familiar shade.

He was not worried by the fact he had killed Jones; that had been inevitable. They had always shared the knowledge that some day one would cause the death of the other. If any memories harried him now they would come out of the more distant past; their shared past in which he had so many times failed to act decisively, had allowed Jones to dictate the disastrous course of events which had brought them eventually to Norway.

They had met first when Cooper was fourteen, living in a Stepney slum with his mother and the never-ending procession of visiting uncles. Into his world, already distorted in some incomprehensible way, had come this other boy, unknown, unexpected. That he was bad and that he frightened Cooper's mother was immediately obvious. Cooper's attempt to throw out the intruder had earnt him a vicious beating while his mother looked on, screaming helplessly. When the uncle currently sharing their house had tried to interfere Jones had produced a knife. Jones stayed, the uncle left. That night the mother drank too much and blurted out the frightful truth that Andy and the blond monster were brothers. Even across so many years, across so many deaths including Jones', Cooper felt again the pain of that terrible wound. He had burst into tears, something he had not done since infancy, while Jones sat in the only comfortable chair and laughed at him. He wished he had killed him then. From that moment, in some horrible way, they were trapped together; hating each other but strangely dependent on each other in their rotten world.

Within six months they had established a reign of terror in their neighbourhood.

They intimidated and robbed young and old; smashed windows, locks and faces indiscriminately. It was a familiar pattern for Jones; a new world for Cooper. But they were equally determined to outdo the other in the scope and viciousness of their running fight with the rest of the world. When the law caught up with them they were separated for a time because Jones received a much severer sentence as a result of his previous record and greater age. When Jones was released he found Cooper waiting for him. Cooper could not explain why he had waited. They returned to their former pattern of life together, but this time it did not last for long.

Jones had been home for about two weeks when, during one of their evening rows with their mother, Jones struck her. It was the signal for which both young thugs had been waiting. Cooper had his hands on Jones's throat before his mother's cry of pain had ceased to make the windows rattle. They fought for about five minutes before the uncle sharing their mother's bed that week had rushed downstairs and jumped them. Fortunately, he was a very strong man, and Cooper and Jones had been too busy killing each other to set on him. He had taken his chance, grabbed them both and slammed their heads together. They had dropped unconscious in the midst of the debris. When they recovered the uncle had disappeared and their mother was half-heartedly rummaging through the wreckage of her home. Then she turned them out of the house so she could clean up; but when they sneaked back two hours later they found her drunk on the floor. 'Silly cow,' sneered Jones, and this time Cooper offered no defence.

A week later, the uncle who had thumped them was found dead on a patch of waste ground. He had been coshed from behind and then very carefully kicked to death so that almost every bone in his body had been broken. The police questioned the boys for hours; they and the mother knew that one or both of them had done it. Cooper knew the killer was Jones. Jones was sure they couldn't pin anything on him, he had been so careful. He was unmarked and the cosh, his suit and his shoes had been burnt.

When things quietened down a bit Cooper suggested they move on to a new place and Jones agreed. They went to Birmingham and three days later Jones beat an elderly tobacconist to death for the sum of four pounds, seven shillings. Cooper could still remember his resentful surprise at his rush of concern, not for the victim but for Jones. This must have distorted his judgement still further because instead of abandoning him he helped him.

They travelled to Liverpool and, at Cooper's instigation, made enquiries about joining the army. The imminence of war made the army eager to accept volunteers, and since no one knew they had been in Birmingham they were not connected with that killing. As for the dead uncle, the police did nothing. They had only suspicion to act upon and they were finding less and less time for hopeless cases now that all aliens had to be traced, interviewed and cross-checked.

So the army took them and they discovered that much of what had previously been regarded as unlawful conduct was now encouraged. The British Army had picked two winners.

Cooper dragged himself into the present, looked at his watch and the sky: too late to find an alternative hideout now. He sat with his back against a rock and looked blankly across the cold, grey land. Of course it had not been quite as easy as that. The army had asked some questions, especially when they volunteered for special jobs. Most of the queries had been dropped once the two men had effectively demonstrated their exceptional gifts for killing and sabotage. This acceptance, this success cemented still further the relationship between them.

Their hatred for each other remained a vital passion within them, but ideas of killing each other were shelved as long as they could kill Germans instead. Gradually, Cooper had come to realise that he was the cleverer member of the team and also, to his cost, the more sensitive member. He found difficulty in accepting the idea that he and Jones really did need each other. Jones, on the other hand, appeared unaware of the strangeness of their relationship; he was too busy and too happy killing to worry over trifles. He was enjoying what the British press would have described as 'a good war'.

Cooper spread out his sleeping bag as he reflected on their service together. He knew that if he had worked alone, or with anyone but Jones, he would quickly have demonstrated his ineptitude and unsuitability for guerrilla warfare. But Jones had taken care of that point; it was his efficiency which prevented Cooper escaping. He had made sure of success so often that Cooper was trapped with the protector he loathed. Now he was free he was wallowing in fear and anxiety. Worse still was the unexpected approach of grief. Enraged by this, and by the knowledge he could not escape his pursuing memories, he dived into his sleeping bag and shut his eyes. Eventually, he slept.

He was awakened by the midday sun

burning the back of his neck. He rolled on to his back, shading his eyes with his forearm. Absolute silence. No one had found him. He lay still, drained of all feeling, all emotion. Sleep had intervened just in time, giving him the pause his mind needed.

He began to think around his freedom and found nothing to impede him. He sat up suddenly, clutching his aching head. Somewhere at the back of his consciousness someone, something, debated with him whether the change of mood was the effect of the sun, of sleep or of madness.

He shrugged his way out of his sleeping bag and took a long, cool drink of water. The slopping of the water in the bottle reminded him of the clear stream where he had filled it. Clear stream, hot sun, no one to listen to, no one giving orders, so why sit in damp clothing? He stood up, slightly dizzy with the uncertainty of this new freedom. He could do what he liked. Being alone gave him powers he had never dreamed of possessing.

He ripped off his damp clothes and stood naked, arms outstretched, feeling the sun soaking into him, driving out the damp, the cold, the stiffness of a lifetime.

Drunk with sunlight he danced a mad jig round the rocks; skipping, jumping, leaping. He collapsed laughing on his bed. He had realised how funny he looked: white body, black face. The sun struck him again on the neck. 'Better get dressed, ready for the off. No, don't. Let clothes dry out. Who's to know? Andy boy — you're barmy.'

His wild chattering stopped, he squatted on his haunches. The devastating implications of his freedom smote him like the sun. He need not go to the dam at all. Whatever would the Major do if he did not appear? He could tell him any old tale; better still, he could invent a story that raised Hurst's suspicions just enough for him to kick him out of Special Operations without bringing any specific charges. What an idea! His mind spun at the intoxicating thought of really fucking up the whole issue. Just think of the right story; that was all he had to do. Lurking at the back of his mind was the knowledge he could not or would not do it, but that made no difference. It was the idea that was so marvellous. Whatever would Hurst say if he didn't turn up?

* * *

Hurst was also lying in the sun but he was not enjoying it. He was far too busy worrying to enjoy himself. It was his own failure that worried him most. Dawn had found him half a mile short of his objective; not a great distance in itself but it might as well have been twenty miles. That half mile was a great wilderness of scree clinging to the precipitous slopes above the camp. He would have to cross it tonight before he could make his last move to the dam. It was not a pleasant prospect and he had a whole day to think of it.

He knew all the reasons why he had failed to complete the journey. He had taken too long crossing the fiord; then heavy rain slowed him as he climbed the mountain-side; the rain had also reduced visibility and made it difficult for him to find the supply dump. The last stage of the journey was back down the hill into the valley, but he had not been able to make up for lost time; it had been too dangerous to hurry. But the root cause of his difficulties had been his own anxiety. He had been so anxious to insure against every conceivable mishap he had overloaded himself. He had realised this as soon as he got into the dinghy and took his pack from Reilly but he had decided to press on. When he reached the south shore he had once again considered dumping some of his ammunition but had not done so; every bullet dropped in the fiord was one shot less for distracting the Germans when Joe was in the camp.

The climb to the plateau almost killed him. He had not appreciated how tired he was, had not understood how much he had been weakened by driving himself and his men so hard. The members of the team had made huge demands on his mind and body which were additional to his own demands; in leading them, in driving them, he had taken on the major share of their own fears and weaknesses. When he finally reached the supply dump he was ready to admit he had miscalculated. It was a bitter defeat.

He had been in a dilemma: he had to collect some food in case Cooper had not found his dump, and he had to pick up more explosive in case Cooper failed to reach the dam. By the time he had thrown out some ammunition and replaced it with food and explosive his pack was almost the same weight as when he started. He had forced himself on across the high ground until he reached the valley edge. Then he had started climbing down towards the camp. Even then he might just have reached his objective before dawn but a bad fall slowed him down. His face was cut, his left knee and ankle were twisted, and his left wrist and two fingers of the left hand were smashed. It was the pain of his hand which now prevented him from sleeping.

His own failure made him doubly concerned about Cooper's progress. Cooper had to get to the dam because he himself could not carry out the job alone. Even if his damaged leg held up for the next half-mile his broken hand would prevent him placing the charges properly. A big explosion was no use if it did not cut off the power. He scanned the valley side with his glasses but there was no sign of Cooper. He could not forget Cooper's silence since Jones died, nor the strange smile on his face when they parted at the Lion Head. He swung his glasses up to the cave but there was no sign of life, and the cave itself was hidden by the sloping ledge in front of it.

They must be pretty comfortable up there, he thought. Hope Joe manages that fool Harding. Bet he still believes he was selected because he's a top man. If he was that good they'd never have risked him. He's a second rate expendable type — poor chap. On top of him I then go and pick Cooper! I didn't know how much the job was loaded against me. Now everything depends on Cooper. If he fluffs it then Joe'll try and go it alone while Harding goes for the lab. block. Cooper must pull it off. Must. Wouldn't be so bad if Jones was with him but he's not much good by himself any more. The end of Jones was the end of him. Weird how Cooper finished him off. Wanted to. Bloody odd pair. Somehow, being half-brothers didn't come into it. No affection there and certainly not queers. Tied together by something else: mutual hatred? It could be that, I've met it before.

Joe's the only normal one left! He'll be all right if Cooper does his job. Andy bloody Cooper I'll get you the softest job, the juiciest woman, your own choice of posting, if you pull this off. Just be there, you sod. Be there!

15

Reilly and Harding crouched on the ledge and watched the advancing night. The massed ranks of conifers had exchanged the liquid green of day for the black of night. The last trace of sunset purple had vanished from the great black rock faces across the water and the camp had vanished in the blackness. Only the dam could still be identified as a slightly lighter strip of stone on the hillside. A breeze had sprung up driving small, dark clouds westward towards the sunset. The high clouds in the vanguard still glowed with magenta tints, but those overhead and in the east were more sombre colours: greys to dark greys to black.

'Two minutes,' whispered Reilly. In two minutes they and their plans would be tested, tested to destruction. Harding thought of all the work he and Reilly had done in the last three hours: checks and counter-checks of procedures, of equipment they were taking with them, of equipment prepared for their return. Reilly had even packed Harding's rucksack for him so it would be waiting ready for their dash to the coast.

'One minute,' said Reilly. It was oddly comforting to know that far away, Cooper and Hurst were also checking the time, were also ready to move. How were they feeling? Harding shivered in the cold breeze.

'Now,' said Reilly, jerking Harding out of his reverie. 'Ready? Go!' Reilly grinned as he reminded them both of their first day on the assault course. He led the way along the narrow ledge, the ledge that had first brought them to the cave. Then he stepped boldly down into the chasm of the world beneath them. Harding plunged after him, started to slide and cannoned into Reilly's legs. They both skidded about twenty feet down the slope, Reilly cursing softly all the way, until they came to a jarring stop against the bole of a stunted pine.

'Trying to kill us both, are you?' snarled Reilly. 'That's the only steep bit without a rope to help us. You would slip there, you clumsy sod!'

'Sorry,' whispered Harding. He felt Reilly's comment was more than justified. He was only carrying his Schmiesser and that was across his back so he had both hands free, but Reilly was carrying his guns, a full pack, and had his deep pockets crammed with grenades. Once Harding had given him that initial push he must have thought that either he would never stop sliding or that he would be blown to pieces as he bounced down the mountain-side.

'Once we're in the trees it'll be bloody dark, old son. So stick close to me and keep your wits about you. You know what to look for: a faint light at the base of the trees. On the very steepest sections use the ropes I've fixed up. Don't try and be clever and manage without, I don't want you having another go at shoving me head first into the trunk of a bloody great tree. You can try breaking my neck when we get back to Blighty. Come on.'

Cautiously, they walked down into the blackness of the forest, glad to be out of the cutting breeze and surrounded by the firm hand-holds of many tree trunks — the innumerable pillars supporting an unseen roof. Harding looked upwards but could see nothing beyond the lowest branches. The dark cathedral of the trees held them secure under an invisible canopy of branches; only the wind soughing in the pointed crowns confirmed that the great green arches were there above their heads.

Whenever they reached a particularly steep section of the mountain-side Reilly paused at the tree to which he had tied a rope and pushed the slack cord into Harding's hands. Then he stepped down into the depths, pulling the rope tight so that Harding felt it quivering in his hands as he hesitated to follow. Then he too plunged downwards with only the rope to save him. The slopes were never so steep that he actually hung from the rope, but it would have been impossible to descend without it; he could not place his feet so securely on the invisible rocks beneath him that he dared to release the rope. As he slid down the mountain-side, banging his thighs, scraping his knuckles, he wondered how Reilly and Hurst had ever managed to make that first descent without fixed ropes to guide them. Even for them, it must have been appallingly difficult to carve out this route at night.

His thoughts were abruptly cut short as he banged his shins painfully on the tree to which Reilly had just tied the lower end of the rope.

'Noisy bugger,' Reilly hissed in his ear. 'I'll leave the ropes tied at the bottom ends for when we come back. No one's likely to come this way in the next few hours. Now, the next bit's pretty easy. I'll lead. You keep your eyes skinned for fluorescent paint.'

The less steep sections proved to be the most frightening. In the first place the thick blanket of pine needles deadened all sound and gave Harding the impression he had lost Reilly. Worse still, the dry needles made a treacherous surface to move down and he covered much of the distance sliding on his backside. He felt he was losing his way; the only certainty being that he was sliding *down* the hill.

He was very relieved to catch sight of the eerie glow of fluorescent paint as he slithered past a tree. He grabbed at the next tree trunk as he slid past and nearly dislocated his right shoulder. He pulled himself upright and lurched on down the slope, staggering from tree to tree, following the pale glow-worms that marked the trail.

He found Reilly waiting for him at the top of the next roped section. Neither of them spoke but Harding felt Reilly's disapproval lancing towards him through the darkness. He supposed his clownish progress must seem very noisy to someone who moved so silently. He shrugged his shoulders, then wished he had not; the right one really hurt. Thankfully, he clasped the rope Reilly thrust at him and launched himself down the slope. He was relieved to feel the vibrations of Reilly's progress telegraphed back to him through the rope.

At last he heard the sound of small waves lapping the shore, felt Reilly's arm checking his progress for the last time. Then they were standing on the tiny beach hemmed in between trees and water. Although there was no moon he could see more clearly than in the vaulted blackness of the trees. He could see the wavelets rolling towards him out of the night when they were still thirty yards away, could see the main planes of Reilly's face as he turned to look at him. Other impressions crowded in: Reilly's heavy breathing, the cold breeze off the water slapping their sweat-studded faces, the black trees behind, black water ahead.

Harding knelt to drink, felt Reilly's hand on the nape of his neck, heard him whisper in his ear, 'Make a sound and I'll drown you.' Almost a caress, yet both knowing he would do just that if it became necessary. Harding staggered to his feet, felt Reilly's arm steady him. 'Not so fit after all?' Reilly said. 'Never mind we made bloody good time with you falling on me so often. Sit down and rest.'

He sat with his back against Reilly's pack and watched the small, stocky figure of his companion as he stalked about the beach. He filled the water bottles and hid them at the forest edge, at the base of the tree to which the last rope was tied. Then he gouged out a line in the sand with his heel; the line pointed at the tree. 'To tell us where to start our climb if we're in a terrible hurry,' he whispered. 'No one else is likely to find it tonight.' Harding thought this a remarkable understatement; he could not imagine anyone else ever finding this tiny, isolated, forest-locked strip of sand.

Reilly knelt beside him, opened the pack and dragged out the two-man dinghy. He carried it to the water's edge, unpacked it and then inflated it. The faint hissing of the gas seemed to shatter the silence like a November fifth rocket, but no answering sounds reached out to them from across the fiord. He checked the dinghy for leaks by walking it into the water; then he dragged it back out again on to the beach. He walked across to Harding, water squelching in his boots, his teeth chattering. 'Water's freezing,' he groaned. 'God knows what it's like in winter. Almost makes me wish I'd had to use the emergency air pump just to get warm again.'

They checked their weapons, checked safety catches, checked their wire cutters, checked the collapsible paddles, checked the two compasses, checked their watches, checked each other's blacking. Harding watched Reilly as he screwed the silencer on to his Luger, put it back into its long, waterproof holster and then pushed the gun down into his anorak, carefully drawing the zip right up to his chin. Lastly, he carried his pack containing the air pump into the trees and dumped it with the water bottles. 'Time to go, sonny. You get in the dinghy with the guns and I'll push you off.'

They both got wet feet trying to keep the Schmiessers dry while making a silent launching, but eventually they began to drift away from the beach with its scars of footprints and the line Reilly had drawn in the sand. With difficulty they wriggled around until they were lying side by side. It would have been a tight fit anyway, but with their figures swollen by the ammunition and bombs they were carrying they were jammed tight against the heaving bulbous sides of the dinghy. They put the compass on the floor between their arms and, with one paddle each, set a slow, steady course due east.

They had not travelled very far before they began to regret their choice of position. The inadequately insulated floor of the dinghy did not keep out the cold. They could feel the freezing touch of the water groping for them through the double skin of rubber, reminding them that only that rubber lay between them and the icy plunge into the deep, dark fiord. They tried to escape the worst effects of the bitter cold by turning sideways but found they were too tightly wedged to move.

At last, they could not bear the agony of the cold burning into their testicles any longer; they tore themselves free of each other and curled up in a crouch position, face to face like a twin foetus. Unfortunately, their struggles had forced their low-riding boat even lower and they spent a miserable five minutes bailing out. All this they had trained for, but never in waters so cold.

They covered the middle stage of the

crossing half-kneeling, half-crouching in an inch of water. As their knees got colder digging into the sagging rubber they seemed to get sharper, threatening to perforate the bottom of the dinghy. Their slow, silent paddling did not keep them warm and they could feel their blood circulating more and more slowly, while the water climbed up through their clothing like ink rising in blotting paper.

They approached their landfall, stopped paddling and drifted silently towards the shore. As they waited to discover exactly where they were they felt the cold fumbling into their hearts, drawing out the last reserves of body heat. If they raised themselves off the bottom of the dinghy the raw wind knifed into their faces, if they crouched low the icy water heaved itself up at them through the dinghy floor. The coldest air in the world was sliding down into the valley to rest on the coldest water — and they were frigidly sandwiched between the two.

'Turn right,' moaned Reilly, through numbed lips. 'Now steady — drift now.' They had found their landing point, could see the mud of the delta edge just ahead of them. Their rate of drifting was slowed by the cold wind but at last they attained the shore. They were thirty yards from the perimeter fence, and that meant not more than forty yards from the shadows of the buildings inside the wire; shadows in which guards might be waiting.

They would have to leave the dinghy without standing up, without splashing, without a sound. They had to prepare their bodies for this as well as their minds; a slow, agonising massage of knee joints, elbows, wrists, was essential. So absorbed were they in their private anguish that they nearly refloated the dinghy by moving too energetically against the dinghy bottom as it slithered back and forth on the soft mud.

Reilly pushed his mouth against Harding's ear, his breath no warmer than the east wind. 'Now — follow — drag dinghy — keep low.'

Reilly carefully strapped his Schmiesser across his shoulders, then very slowly edged his way over the side of the dinghy, slipped into three inches of water and crawled through it to firm ground. When Harding followed he nearly shouted aloud as the cold water sucked him down. He crawled forward, pulling the dinghy with him until it was firmly grounded. All this had to be done painfully slowly to avoid splashing water about. He carried out the manoeuvre lying in glutinous mud which sucked at his body but offered little purchase for probing toecaps and frozen fingers. Furthermore, he had to stay face down for fear of getting mud in the gun on his back. He almost laughed hysterically at the crazy idea the mud would freeze solid on them, locking them in strange postures until, at dawn, the Germans would find them and mercifully chip them out of their casts. He put his head down and crawled doggedly after Reilly.

The slow wriggling forward over rough ground began to thaw them out; numbed knees struck hard against tussocks of grass, grass unyielding and brittle, rasping across frozen faces. Reilly halted so Harding stopped. Then on again, then halting as Reilly stared fixedly at the guard leaning against the wall beside large double doors. At last Reilly sank into the turf and signalled Harding to come up beside him.

They were ten yards from the wire and in line with those double doors leading into building J; the building they had scrutinised so carefully from the Lion Head. The guard appeared quite relaxed, not bothering to march up and down; not bothering to walk across to the wire. The wire was fascinating: they could see the insulators holding it clear of the posts; even in the darkness the white insulators stood out clearly. No one electrifies fences round rest homes for war wounded.

This new knowledge, this hopeful, frightening sign helped them survive the long wait; a long wait lying face down, head resting on arms; a long wait fighting off the stiffening of frozen limbs and worrying that they would be unable to move quickly when they had to. The only exercise they could risk was the gentle flexing of muscles: legs, shoulders, arms, hands and fingers.

They waited with their wire cutters on the ground in front of them, their Schmiessers on their backs with slings round their left shoulders. Reilly held his Luger in his right hand with the barrel resting on his left forearm. Getting themselves so prepared had taken several minutes of painful, fumbling movements. Now, lying with their heads on their arms, they could watch the progress of the minute hands of their watches under the short cuffs of their gloves. The hands moved slower and slower as 01.15 hours came nearer.

01.15. They were tensed, ready. Harding could feel the toes of his boots sinking into the soft ground as he braced himself. He gripped the wire cutters with his right hand; and pressed down on the ground with his left. Out of the corner of his eye he could see Reilly had raised the Luger and was aiming at the guard's chest. 01.15.

Nothing happened.

There was no explosion, no brilliant flash of light, no clattering fall of broken piping, no sudden, uncontrolled rush of water. Hurst had so carefully briefed them that they knew the sounds to expect. But they were sounds that echoed hollowly in their imagination. The reality was silence.

16

Cooper lay in the rocks thirty yards from the guard hut at the north end of the dam. Next to him lay his pack bulging with extra food, ammunition and explosives taken from the dump in the hills. His Schmiesser lay on the ground but with its barrel resting on the edge of the pack and clear of the mud and wet grass. He would only need it if things went wrong. The job was one for knives or silenced pistols.

Slowly, painfully, he moved his left wrist towards his face, then using his right hand he pulled down his left glove and looked at his watch. Five minutes left. He wondered if he would be able to move at the crucial moment; the damp cold had stiffened him as much as his fear. Only his hands were ready; he had been flexing his fingers in his gloves, keeping the blood moving sluggishly into his finger tips. He looked ahead, at the guards on the dam;

they were too near for him to risk easing his cramped legs. He had to wait, and when he did move it would have to be quickly, purposefully; no time for limbering up.

Voices from the dam. The two guards had met in the centre and were talking. Their black silhouettes appeared to merge and Cooper could no longer identify them as two persons. There was no moon and dark clouds wheeled overhead, but the sunken sun was too near the horizon for the night to be completely black. At thirty yards it was possible to identify familiar shapes, but two men huddled together, sharing body heat and reminiscence, appeared to Cooper to be an amorphous patch of shadow.

The men moved apart and walked towards opposite ends of the dam. Cooper knew that the man walking towards him would stop at the hut, turn round and walk slowly back to his companion who would be returning from the south end of the dam. The pattern of their patrolling was fixed, but unfortunately the timing of it was completely unpredictable. Sometimes they talked for several minutes when they met, at other times they did not stop to speak but immediately turned away from each other and repeated their short march.

Hurst would act when they were at opposite ends of the dam; he would go for his man just as he turned round to face his comrade. Perhaps the other guard would see Hurst rising up out of the rocks, but before he could cry out either Cooper's knife would be in his back or a bullet from the silenced Luger would split his brain.

Timing was everything. Cooper knew he could rely on Hurst to strike when the moment best suited them both. If anything went wrong Hurst would expect him to take care of the two men sleeping in the hut. If there was so little noise the sleepers did not wake, then they would not be dealt with until the shocking noise of the explosion brought them reeling from the hut. If noise betrayed them too soon he and Hurst could still blow the dam because it would take nearly half an hour for men to climb the tortuous path from the camp.

The really disastrous consequence of raising the alarm before the dam was blown would be that Reilly and Harding would find an alert enemy waiting for them when they tried to cut through the wire. The first sound to be heard in the valley must be the explosion cutting off the power supply.

He looked again at his watch. It was almost time. In one minute it would be 01.00 hours. Had five minutes really passed? He pressed the watch to his ear; the faint murmur of passing time was reassuring. He looked at the watch face again — part of it had vanished. Gently, he rubbed it with his sleeve and the figures became clear. He must have got blacking on it when he held it against his ear. The fact the watch was working need not mean anything. It might be slow! He had to get into position.

He rose to a crouch. It was agony: his knees locked with cramp, his thighs stiffened like posts. Then, in spite of the pain, he moved forward silently, came to the hut, slipped into its deep shadow. He stood there, breathing shallowly, stifling the cry of pain blocking his throat. The sudden movement had sent molten fire through every limb, every vein; he felt as if every joint in his body had been dislocated. Even gearing his mind to the demands of the next few seconds did not diminish his awareness of pain.

He drew his knife, black-bladed, dull-edged, needle-tipped. He weighed it affectionately in his right hand. His left hand caressed the butt of his silenced Luger as it lay in the deep, oiled holster that had been stitched into the place of an ordinary pocket on his left thigh. He knew that in spite of the extra length of the silencer he could draw the gun faster than any actor in a cowboy film. But he preferred the knife.

He crouched at the corner of the hut and very slowly allowed his head to move forward so he could see the dam. He was safe there as long as none of the guards made for the latrine in the rocks behind the hut. It was to avoid being discovered in this way that he had spent so long lying on the rain-soaked ground thirty yards away. He was now only a few yards from the middle of the little dam. When the guard he must deal with reached the end of his measured walk, he would be the length of the hut plus two yards from Cooper. Cooper knew that that distance was exactly seven, quick, unimpeded paces. He waited for Hurst.

The two guards were talking again. Then they turned and walked away from each other. Cooper's man walked slowly towards him. Cooper breathed in, crouched in the pitch black of the hut's shadow, knife ready. The man drew nearer. Cooper was perfectly balanced on his toes. The man was ten paces from the hut, then five, then four, then three. He stopped, slowly turned. Cooper strained forward, watching the dark shape of the other guard: Hurst's target. The other guard had stopped and, turning slowly, faced towards Cooper. Cooper knew he would not be seen unless he moved suddenly. Nothing happened. The guards stood looking towards each other along the narrow path of the dam. Nothing happened.

Cooper's guard began to stroll away from him towards his colleague. Hurst had left it too late. Cooper sank back into the crouch position once more. His chest felt as if it would burst. His breathing seemed too loud; a harsh, betraying rattle. He was shaking. It would be next time then. Not now but next time they parted. He forced himself not to wipe the sweat from his face; dared not risk removing blacking, showing pale skin. Another time check: 01.03. Can't let things drag on much longer, he thought. Explosion due at 01.15. This time, Major. Now or never. This time. Come on. Now!

Yet again the guards parted. Cooper held the knife hard against his thigh, willing the Major to come out of the rocks. Nothing happened. He was suddenly aware he was standing exposed, away from the side of the hut, standing with his mouth open. He froze. The guard had his back to him again. Tempting target; he could not miss. He took a pace forward, then stopped. He could do nothing until the man on the far side of the dam fell to the ground, or until he saw Hurst's shadow closing in on him. But still nothing happened. The guard began walking away from him. Cooper slumped back into the shadow.

He stared, unseeing now, across the dam. Faint outlines of distant rocks, motionless sentinels, stared back as they had stared across hundreds of years. But no shadow moved. No sign, no sign; only the muttering of the waves against the dam and the slap of the guards' feet on the concrete. This was worse than Jones. Something had happened to the Major. It must have done.

It was 01.08. If Hurst appeared now they would only just have time to blow the pipes by 01.15 hours. The two guards stood firmly in the middle of the dam, their backs to the hand rail that gave some protection from plunging down the dam face into the camp below. If the Major appeared now the guards would have time to call, or even if they fell backwards down the dam without screaming, their bodies and their weapons would make too much noise as they clattered down on to the camp.

Cooper looked at his watch again. The hands, once so slow moving, were now racing round the face, were just passing 01.11. The Major was not coming. Something terrible had happened. Cooper found himself screaming silently, opening and shutting his mouth. He was drenched with sweat. He could not stand there any longer. He slipped swiftly back to his starting point and flung himself down beside his pack.

They had failed. It was all over. The Major, of all people, had let them down. Cooper groaned softly, banged his fist hard on the butt of his gun. Then he lay absolutely still. The real meaning of this disaster suddenly burst into his mind with the fierce acid light of a white flare.

He had to do it alone.

He had to go in alone; he could not avoid it. Reilly and Harding were lying down there at the boundary fence waiting for the pipes to be blown. And nothing was going to happen, except that those two down there would die in a frantic effort to operate alone. Nothing would happen at the dam unless he made it happen.

He pulled his knees up to his chest, stuffed his gloved hands into his mouth. It was the end of him if he went in alone. But it had to be done, and done now. He straightened his legs, rolled on to his stomach, half-stood, his legs folded and he fell back to the ground.

Eventually, he got himself into a kneeling position. Then he knew exactly what to do.

He laid his machine-gun to one side and opened his pack. He took out everything except the charges; these he set up in the pack, adjusting the arm and magnet that would hold the charges in position. Then he checked the roll of wire, made sure it would unroll swiftly, would not snag or catch. Checked his pistol and knife. Left the iron rations, the water, the spare ammunition with the machine-gun. Final check: pistol on safety and placed in pack on top of roll of wire, detonators ready but not finally set, pack closed, knife in sheath. Very cautiously, he worked his arms through the pack straps and adjusted it on his back. Then he was ready. If the Major showed now he would be too late. He began to move forward without being conscious of any decision to start.

He crawled steadily towards the dam, but this time turned away from the hut. Then he waited until the guards met in the centre of the dam. He crossed the path, over the edge and lay flat, out of sight. He was now below the level of the hut, slightly below the level of the top of the dam. In front of him was the cliff that plunged vertically two hundred feet to the camp. If the guards moved too soon the man approaching the hut would see him. Then he heard voices. It was all right: they were still talking.

He wriggled forward, placed his hands round the end stanchion of the guard rail that ran across the dam, and lowered himself into space. He was hanging down the face of the dam with his hands round the bottom of the stanchion. The weight of the pack nearly tore his hands loose. Then his arms flexed, took the strain and he hung there. He could feel the concrete against his toes, could feel the sloping face of the dam. That sloping face was tempting; would tempt him to trust it more as he got tired. The further he went the more it would seem the dam face was a gently sloping wall which would support him if he released his grip; when in fact it would barely check his falling body. The only good thing about his position was that he was sheltered from the wind.

Now he had to move. It was six feet to the next post and he could not reach it. Even without the weight of the pack pulling him down and away from it he could not reach it. He knew he must work his way along the dam by making short, swinging movements, moving his right hand to the right, and then bringing his left hand to join it. He estimated that three firm movements would bring him to the next post.

He was wrong. When his grasping right hand missed the post after three 'steps' he nearly fell. The fourth move was right. He grasped the post with both hands. The luxury of a firm handhold was a blessed relief after swinging by his fingertips from the concrete lip of the dam. He hung there, motionless; forehead pressed against the cold, rough-textured concrete.

He hung there relaxed until a faint scraping noise reached him. His feet, apparently detached from him, way down in the blackness below, were trying to find some purchase on the concrete. He was suddenly angry, turned his toes down and just hung there. He deliberately closed his mind to the pains developing within his tortured body, deliberately rejected the knowledge that the pipes to the power house led down from the far side, Hurst's side of the dam. He could not bear to think how far he had to travel.

Just when he knew he would fall he heard footsteps; the sound for which he was praying. The guards had separated once more and were moving to the ends of the dam. He could move now the centre was unguarded. The next six feet were easy; he swung smoothly to the next stanchion. Footsteps again. He quelled his harsh breathing, made sure he could reach his knife with his right hand, then hung there. Then he heard the guards' voices. He knew he could hang on while they chatted but Harding and Reilly would have to wait as well. Perhaps Hurst was waiting.

He gradually became aware of a curious feeling of discomfort, queasiness; almost like sea-sickness. His head was throbbing. He felt as if he was lying flat on the gently sloping dam face and it was heaving under him. It's breaking up. The Major's done something to it already. Gently sloping walls don't move like . . . Christ! It's me, me — not gently sloping but nearly upright! He was relaxing his hold, the wall had won, deceived him in to thinking he could lie against it. His grip tightened again. He pulled himself in against the concrete, rasped his unshaven chin on the stone. The wall stopped moving. Somewhere, in the back of his mind, he acknowledged how much the last few days had exhausted him.

The guards met in the centre of the dam and, this time, did not stop to chat.

He moved fast, almost ignoring the chance of betraying his presence. Then he hung again. The wall heaved quite gently, as if rippling waves on the far side, were transmitting their motion to the concrete and thence to his head. This was wrong. He had to keep fully alert. He blinked as sweat trickled into one eye; almost made the fatal error of putting his hand to his eyes. Checked, held on tight.

Again he moved, and again, on and on, wondering if he would ever cross the dam. It might be easier to go back. Then he looked down and there, between his braced legs and the wall, in that triangle of night, was wedged the fat, voluptuous, curved shape of an iron pipe. He had nearly succeeded.

The problem now was that the pipe was three feet below him. He had to drop down, but how? More important — when? He closed his eyes, once more visualised the dam. He saw the model, saw the real thing: the view from the Lion Head. He was not in the centre of the dam but near the right hand end, the south end. He must wait for the guards to meet in the middle. When he heard them talking he could drop down, not on to that fat pipe but between it and its neighbour.

He swung by his hands once more until he was positioned above the space between the two pipes. If he could drop straight down, then before he bounced off the pipes, those smooth, steeply plunging pipes, and fell to his death, he could wedge his legs in the gap between them.

Mentally, he prepared himself. He had to leave go, start to fall, but fall into that gap which was only about eighteen inches wide, keeping his body and head forward against the dam. If he leant backwards out into space he would be trapped by his feet with his body hanging out backwards over the camp.

He was ready, waiting for the voices of the guards. If he could not hear them he would have to pull himself up to the level of the dam top and see where they were standing before he could let himself go. Then everything was all right because he could hear them laughing together.

He fell, feet into gap, nearly screaming

279

in agony as his left knee cap was jammed flat between the pipe and his right leg. He resisted the temptation to change his position, concentrating instead on pressing against the dam so he did not topple back, outwards and downwards into the black void. When he had gained his balance he braced himself between the pipes and slowly turned sideways. He made a perfect wedge with his legs; he could actually sit or half-lean on one pipe. He was safe.

He rested until he heard the guard pass above him. While he waited he became aware of a faint drumming against his legs. It was the water gushing down inside the pipes: arterial blood to the camp below. The artery would soon be severed. He checked the time and once more disbelieved his watch. 01.17 hours. He was suddenly immensely pleased with himself; he had done that journey in not much more than five minutes. It had felt like hours. All the same, he was working behind time now, and down below him Reilly and Harding would be pretty worried.

Down below — he dared not look down. He looked up instead, up at the edge of the dam above him, about six feet above his head. Could he get back? He could if he stood on top of the pipes where they entered the wall. There was a very small ledge in the concrete, about two inches wide, if only he could push up. He checked himself abruptly. The charges first.

The most difficult part was removing his pack. Twice he nearly fell; only his jammed thighs saved him. He kept his mind closed to the searing pain in his damaged knee. At last he was free of his pack and stopped struggling. His arms throbbed in the agony of release; so much so that his hands shook uncontrollably. Then he steadied himself once more. I'm doing bloody well, really, and doing it alone. The Major might be watching. Jones. No Jones. Mind on the job. Mind on the job. Check once more all set. Now get out — taking wires and switch. Good old Jerry made a neat switch. Get your own back in a minute. Now to get up somehow.

He braced himself on his thighs and forced the pack between the pipes. The powerful magnet held it in position while he screwed the expanding arm tighter and tighter. The arm extended from the pack until it was jammed rigidly across the gap between the two pipes. That was the answer to his last worry. He could stand on the pack itself. The arm would not give until the explosion forced the two pipes apart.

He checked the terminals on the switch box. He checked there was plenty of wire and that it ran free and clear of his legs. He checked his pistol and transferred it to the front of his anorak ready for when he dealt with the guards. The switch box he put into the deep holster pocket so that the wires hung free of his body. He was going up and through the guards now; no question of swinging back to the side of the dam. There was not enough strength left for the return journey, or even for the shorter journey to the south end of the dam.

He took a deep breath, forced himself up with his hands and got his feet on to the pack. It was rock safe as he thrust down with his feet. Then he bit his lip in agony as his knee gave way. He knew he had hurt it, did not know he had smashed it. He swayed forward against the dam and his pistol butt rattled loudly on the concrete.

He hurled himself upwards just as the guards shouted. He grabbed the edge of the dam, pulled himself up, the pistol butt caught, he wrenched himself free and felt the pistol go. He never heard it clattering down the dam face, alerting the camp guards below. He rolled under the rail on to the top of the dam. A shot smashed into the concrete, sharp splinters gouged his face. He heard men running, looked up, saw raised guns, knew his knife was useless, felt a bullet smash his hip, pulled the switch box against his chest, disengaged safety and turned the little key.

17

Harding and Reilly lay side by side, their minds as numbed as their bodies. Hurst had said there might be a slight delay if something unexpected cropped up, but neither of them had really believed such a monstrous thing could happen. One minute passed so slowly they had time to review every conceivable reason for the delay.

The second minute of waiting their bodies gave reminders of their own difficulties; discomforts increased — the cold grew sharper — a knife in the groin. In spite of this they had to remain motionless but fully alert, waiting for the flash of light from the dam. Reilly dared not lower his pistol but waited frozen in his alertness. They were both praying furiously under their breath, beseeching the Major and God, one and the same at that moment, to act, to end their waiting.

When the second minute completed its

weary passage through their lives Harding felt his head turn very slowly to the left. He knew what was happening: he was trying to look up at the dam; he knew it was a very stupid thing to do but was quite unable to check the movement. He was suddenly aware of a burning sensation running down the side of his body. Something happened in his swimming mind and he was once more in control of himself. He did not turn his head, did not make any move. He was astounded to realise that his companion's anger had actually been communicated to him as a physical sensation.

He must have been mad to move knowing he might attract the guard's attention; mad to try looking at the dam, knowing that the flash of the explosion, if it ever happened, would destroy his night vision. The guard would look up, would die as the flash burnt into his eyes. That bright light would be the last thing he saw. Harding kept his eyes riveted on the guard.

The crack of a rifle shot smashed across the valley, then a second shot;

sounds more frightening than the dull thump of the explosion that followed. Afterwards, Harding was to wonder if he even heard the explosion. It was the brilliant flash of light almost overhead that mattered. Light that showed the guard starting forward raising his head, then falling back as Reilly's first shot ripped into his chest, then jerking back even faster as Reilly's second shot, the riskier head shot, tore home.

The muffled reports of the Luger seemed terribly loud in the instant of time between the explosion itself and the dreadful cacophony that followed; a great mass of sounds engulfing them: debris rattling down the dam face, the harsh shriek of a siren, shouts, slamming doors, pounding feet.

Reilly's hand clamped itself on Harding's shoulder. Wait. Even as he checked there came a vivid blue flash from the power house as a huge jet of water came roaring down on to and through the roof of the building. The siren sobbed and moaned into silence.

They hurled themselves at the fence.

Reilly threw his cutters against it to make sure the wires were dead. Then it was exactly like all their rehearsals. They each made a long, inclined cut meeting at the top, pushed down the triangle of wire and dragged themselves through. Every movement was agony after their long wait in the mud but they had no time to think about either their aches or the sharp, prickling distress of reviving circulation. It was noises that mattered: running feet, more shouting, and then the sound they expected and feared: the steady rumbling of a diesel generator coming into action to give emergency lighting.

They forced the cut wire back into position, then hesitated momentarily as new, unexpected noises slammed against the hillsides. There was a noise like the snapping of giant twigs followed by a loud rumbling that made the ground shake. The explosion had weakened the little dam and it was collapsing. A spotlight flared briefly, probing upward towards the dam, and in the instant before the light was forever extinguished, they saw the waters of the lake come frothing through the shattered dam and down on to the buildings at the base of the cliff. To a background of roaring water, crashing slabs of concrete, screams for help, muffled orders, they dragged the dead guard to the door of the building he had been protecting.

It was all very simple. The doors were not locked. They entered cautiously and found themselves in a small entrance hall. They squeezed the guard's body under a table and put his rifle on top of him. Then they locked the outer door from the inside.

The hall was partitioned off from the rest of the building by wood panel walls, in the top of which were small windows overlooking the rooms adjacent to the hall. Reilly sprang on to a table and looked down into a room where five men were making a lot of noise. In the feeble glow of the emergency lighting he could see the white-coated, white-faced men struggling to carry out what he presumed was an emergency evacuation. They were banging into each other, trying to lock filing cabinets and stuffing what were presumably the most vital files into a large, black bag.

They heard Reilly smash the glass, jerked their heads up, saw him aim and fire, saw the man holding the bag fall at their feet.

'Still!' snarled Reilly.

They could not have moved. The noise of the explosion, the sudden blackout, the bedlam of the collapsing dam, the feeble flicker of emergency lighting, had already softened them up; now the sudden appearance of this black-faced, mud-splashed killer petrified them. They stood rigid, still, trying not to look at their dead colleague. Then the office door opened behind them and Harding stepped into the room. 'I've got them, Sergeant.'

The face at the window disappeared, reappearing at their elbows a moment later. 'Try the bag,' said Reilly.

Harding pulled it out from under the dead man and, as he did so, he saw the face for the first time. Carl. It was Carl. He knew Carl. Terrified, he looked up at the other Germans but they remained strangers to him. A strange twist of fate had led Joe to shoot Carl, the only German known to him, before he had entered the room.

The Germans stared at him as he shuffled through the papers, heard him say, 'It's all here, Joe. They just had time to sort out the best stuff for us.'

'Do we burn the other papers?'

'Yes, Joe. Just in case they haven't put all the key stuff in here.'

'Is it what you thought?'

'Looks like it.'

'Cover them,' said Reilly.

Harding waved the four terrified men back against the wall and pointed his Schmiesser at them. As he did so, Reilly quickly fitted a new silencer to his Luger. They all knew why. Harding and his prisoners looked at each other with mutual dread and horror. One of the Germans had a trickle of vomit running into his collar, another had obviously lost control of his bowels. The other two stood tense, white-faced, watching Reilly and Harding out of shocked eyes. No one looked at the body at their feet.

Harding was praying, 'Be quick, Joe. Please be quick.' But Joe was busy inserting fire grenades in the bottom drawer of each filing cabinet.

'I'm giving us five minutes,' he snapped. Then he kicked the bottom drawers shut and pulled out the top ones. 'Improves the draught.' He grinned viciously. 'Right, Captain. We've time to look round and plant a few more surprise packets. I'll just finish off here. You don't want to question them do you?' Dumbly, Harding shook his head.

Reilly shot the four men through the heart at point blank range. Each shot was a little louder than the one before as the silencer's effectiveness decreased. None of the men cried out and there was very little blood. Reilly was out of the office before the bodies stopped twitching. Harding stood looking down at them.

'Come on,' snarled Reilly.

They burst through the other door leading from the entrance hall and found themselves on a gallery overlooking a complex of machinery linked together by a spaghetti mass of pipes. The place was deserted.

Harding could feel a broad smile spreading uncontrollably across his face. Momentarily, he forgot the horror he had just seen, forgot to tell Reilly he had killed someone he knew.

'Is this good?' whispered Reilly.

'It is. This is primitive stuff. We're well ahead of them if this is the best they can do. They may have better works in other centres.'

'You think that's good, do you? It just means we needn't have come.' Reilly was thinking of the delay in blowing the dam. Something must have happened to the Major and here was this bugger grinning all over his silly face because it was all unnecessary.

'Come on,' said Harding. 'I'll show you where to leave your incendiaries.'

As they placed the last bomb they heard sounds of running water. 'Look at that,' growled Reilly, pointing to the door at the far end of the building. Water was creeping blackly across the floor towards them. 'Jerry never dreamed a flood would come from above the camp, did he? My fire bombs will just about beat the flood I reckon.'

They ran back to the steps, up to the gallery and into the the hall. Reilly put his hand on the lock of the outer door. 'Wait,' he hissed. 'The next bit's the hard part.'

They heard men running past the door, presumably checking the fence. The footsteps did not falter; whoever was inspecting the wire had not spotted the gap. The missing guard was presumed to have carried out orders to move to another section of the camp. It had been a wise precaution replacing the wire so carefully. Then someone tried the door, but finding it locked he turned and ran back the way he had come.

'Let's hope he thinks the building's been evacuated,' said Reilly.

He unlocked the door and as he did so a series of muffled explosions in the office behind them announced that five minutes had passed and the fires had started. Reilly dragged the door open. To their dismay the fence opposite the door was illuminated by some kind of floodlight.

'Just switched it on,' hissed Reilly, 'otherwise they'd've spotted the cuts in the wire. Got to go now. The fires we've started will bring every man in the camp down on us. I'll shoot the light out. You get through the fence as fast as you can.' He was tucking the Luger into his anorak as he spoke, then swinging the Schmiesser off his back. 'I'll bring your gun. You take the bag. When I count three. And don't wait for me.' He glared at Harding.

'Ready, sonny?' Harding nodded. 'Right. One, two three!'

Reilly sprang through the doorway, swinging his gun to the right as he did so. Harding, holding the bag in front of him, took three huge strides and dived into the wire. As his rigid arms drove the bag through the cut wire Reilly's gun blasted out the floodlight. Harding wriggled clear of the hole and fell into the mud. He rolled sideways and looked back at Reilly. There was a burst of fire from the area where the floodlight had been set up and Reilly fell against the fence.

The world went mad. Harding heard himself screaming at Reilly as he groped for the hole in the fence. Harding pushed his arms back through the hole and pulled Reilly into it. 'Come on! Get through. Leave the guns to me!' He shrieked.

'I'm O.K.,' sobbed Reilly and began to climb through.

There was another burst of shooting, this time from the hillside near the south end of the dam. Hurst or Cooper was trying to cover their escape by shooting down into the camp. The Germans were still further demoralised by this new attack and returned the fire half-heartedly. But some kept their heads sufficiently to fire again towards the wire where the two men were struggling to free themselves.

Reilly was hit again before Harding could wrench him out of the wire, but he was able to stagger to the dinghy with Harding. As they ran, Reilly kept muttering, 'It's wrong. Something wrong up there. It's wrong.'

Harding knew what he meant. Not only had the dam been blown at the wrong time and after two shots had been fired, but the covering fire they were getting was coming from the wrong end of the dam. Perhaps there was only one man there now. These thoughts raced through Harding's mind as he pushed Reilly into their dinghy, threw in the bag and guns and pushed off from the shore. Reilly grabbed a paddle as well and, together, they forced their way out across the black water. Behind them the gun battle still raged.

They had travelled about one hundred yards when the bombs went off in the laboratory. A great gout of fire slashed up into the night sky, adding even more colour to the chaos of fires, of flashing lights, and of green and red tracer curling up out of the camp towards the hillside. Then the explosion in the laboratory was answered by an even bigger blast high up on the hillside, in the area from which Hurst or Cooper had been pouring fire into the camp. The Germans, hosing the hill with their tracer fire, must have hit one of the packs of explosive carried by their attackers. The noise rumbled round the hills like a thunderclap.

'They've hit the Major's explosives,' whispered Reilly and he slumped to the bottom of the dinghy. Harding looked back towards the hills and, in the light of the fires, saw that the hillside above the camp was beginning to move.

'It's all right, Joe, I think. It looks as if Hurst is trying to bury the camp.' He watched, appalled as the whole scree slope of the hillside came sweeping down on to the Germans. The southern side of the camp vanished under this terrible avalanche of boulders. The noise was unbearable. He clapped his hands over his ears. 'From earthquake, fire and flood, dear Lord. Dear Lord!'

The whole world, their little boat included, was rocked crazily by the sheer volume of sounds, by the spreading, concentric waves bursting across the fiord from the base of the shattered mountain. What it was like in the camp was beyond human imagining. The cumulative effect of those successive disasters, all totally unexpected, all leaping out of the black night, must have been to destroy utterly any sort of order, any kind of discipline.

Harding turned to Reilly but he lay unconscious in the bottom of the dinghy. For the first time in months of training and action Harding was alone. No one was giving orders. Carefully, he picked up his paddle and began to drag the dinghy and its burden further out into the blackness. Behind him the shooting had stopped. The only sounds now were the steady roar of the water plunging down from the lake, the rapacious crackling of the fires, and the rattling and splashing of the last boulders rolling on to the camp or into the fiord. There was no sign or signal from the mountain-side. Were the two men already moving towards the coast? Were they both alive? Why had Hurst fired from the wrong side of the dam?

★ ★ ★

For Major Alec Hurst neither his great strength, nor his courage, nor his experience had proved sufficient to meet the demands made upon him. Everything had ended for him in futility and waste.

Shortly after he started his last journey on the mountain-side his leg gave way and he fell. When he recovered consciousness he found himself lying on the scree slope with both legs broken. He tried to assess his situation but his brain would not function properly. He supposed he was concussed. He did not immediately suffer much pain; his body was numbed from the waist down.

Some time later, he began to check his equipment. His Schmiesser was lying next to him and was undamaged; his binoculars were inside his anorak and were not broken. But his pack had gone. It must have been torn off his back as he fell and was somewhere on the slopes below him; he knew he would never find it. The only ammunition he possessed was that in the gun and in the spare clips in his pockets. His mind worked out that not only would he never reach the dam but also that he could offer little assistance to his team in the way of a diversion. His mind clouded over again.

It was a long time before he thought to check his watch. It was still working. It shrieked a warning which he scarcely heard: in twenty minutes Cooper would be waiting for him at the dam. With some difficulty he considered this fact and began to relate it to his own position. When he lifted the binoculars to his eyes he discovered he could not see the faint lightness of the lake and of the concrete dam. A low rise ahead of him obstructed the view. He had to move.

He dragged himself forward over a distance of about thirty yards. Twice he fainted; both times the fractured bones in his left leg caught on the sharp edges of boulders. When he could go no further he lay face down and wept with frustration. The agony of being stopped was greater than the waves of pain which now swept through him. A part of his mind knew he had just accomplished something tremendous because he could now see the dam; but it was a hollow victory for him.

Eventually, he was able to work out his position in relation to the dam and the camp. He had spent much of the day studying the buildings and so had a perfect mental picture of the layout.

When two careless Germans left doors open with lights showing he worked out a good fix of his position. Then he looked ahead through his glasses at the lighter coloured patch that was the dam. He was four hundred yards away but his glasses brought him right up to the wall. What happened next depended on Cooper. He had to wait for the least reliable man, excluding Harding, to work out what he had to do. Would he work out anything? Perhaps he would just give up when he realised he had to go in alone. Hurst knew what he would do in Cooper's place but that only heightened the suspense of waiting.

Just when he thought his head would burst he detected a movement on the dam face. He held his breath. The movement was repeated; a dark patch of shadow was moving slowly, very slowly, across the lighter colour of the concrete. It must be Cooper and he was doing the right thing. Hurst fainted again.

His great, broken body released him to consciousness once more. He heard the shots at the dam, shut his eyes against the explosion that consumed Cooper and the guards. He nearly choked. Andy had done it! He had succeeded as brilliantly as Hurst had wished. The man he had doubted had proved as resourceful, as determined, as tough as Joe himself. As good as Joe. Perhaps he could back up Cooper's effort and help Joe. At least he could give some covering fire when it was most needed.

The signal came as a deep red glow within one building. He saw fire licking at the blackout screens on the south side of building J. The light warned him to be ready and also helped him to fix his position more accurately in relation to the camp. He had fallen further down the mountain-side than he had supposed. He wondered where his pack was. Then speculations ended. Only action counted.

He saw the floodlight, realised a building intervened between him and it. He was helpless. He heard Joe shoot it out, then he was shooting as well. First clip sprayed the whole camp. He ignored the fact someone was shooting at him from the far end of the shattered dam.

Changed the magazine, cried out with the pain of his smashed hand, fired the second clip through the windows of the barrack block. Third clip into fuel store; fire started. Big explosion in the laboratory meant Joe had done his job. Tracer coming up at him from the camp, shells striking rocks all round him. A vivid flash, huge blast lifting up.

He died instantly. His pack had only rolled a few yards further down the scree.

He never knew how the scree was wrenched loose from the mountain, how millions of tons of boulders smashed on to the camp or plunged into the water. He never knew his shattered body was carried down into the icy, black fiord; down to a silent, majestic but undiscovered grave. He never knew how a great monument sprang up above him as rocks bore down on him, growing into a great mound that stood clear of the water to mark his submarine grave.

18

Sluggishly, the dinghy moved forward. Harding dug his paddle into the water yet again and dragged Reilly and himself a few yards further west. He was squatting in the stern, paddling on alternate sides of the dinghy as if it were a canoe; but the plump, waddling balloon of a boat did not respond like a canoe. His strength was running out but he kept doggedly pulling; driven by the knowledge that he could do nothing for Reilly until he got him out of the cold, wet dinghy.

In the flickering light of the dying fires he could see Reilly's white face turned up to the night sky. His eyes were closed; he was still unconscious. Then the face vanished as the fires were temporarily doused by the spreading flood waters. Faintly, across the fiord, came the hissing sigh of the drowning flames and when Harding looked over his shoulder he saw a white, cumbersome cloud of steam rising slowly across the beam of a spotlight. A little more light would be welcome when he reached the far side of the fiord and tried to find the beach; he doubted the accuracy of his compass reading and knew he was travelling an erratic course westward. Perhaps the fires would flare up again.

Then suddenly, he was glad the light had diminished. The motor launch was starting up.

His position was quite hopeless. He could not get away even if he dumped Reilly overboard. Self-disgust rose in his throat. Had expediency reduced him to that level? He remembered Anders Rogstad.

The only way to lighten the boat was to throw out the guns; if he did that and was then caught he would be unable to fight. His rising panic was matched by the rising volume of noise from the approaching motor boat.

He flung the paddle into the bottom of the dinghy and seized his Schmiesser. He crouched low behind the fat flank of the dinghy; a useless move but he had been thoroughly conditioned. He saw the foaming water at the launch's prow when it was forty yards away. He took careful aim and, as it swept closer, he squeezed the trigger. Nothing happened. His gun did not fire. At the same moment he realised the launch was going past. They had not seen him, did not know of his existence. The launch was being used to ferry helpers from the dormitory block to the camp. That was it! They did not know of his escape from the camp and no one could tell them because the telephone lines were out of action — no electricity.

He sank back on to Reilly's legs and tried to clear his aching head, tried to order his mind; a mind already escaping his control. The launch was going the wrong way to be pursuing him. He should have realised that. He nearly gave himself away by shooting at it. Why had the gun failed? He ran his hands over it and was almost glad Reilly was unconscious. The safety catch was on. He tried to remember when he had put it on and then, cold and exhausted as he was, he felt the hot blood rushing to his face. It had never been off!

He had gone through the whole raid with safety on. When he had covered the men in that office, the men Reilly had so deliberately shot, the safety catch had been on. During the few seconds when Reilly had calmly fitted a new silencer he had kept the Germans covered with a gun that would not have fired. Very, very gently he lowered his gun over the side of the dinghy and released it. Soundlessly, it fell away beneath him in the deep waters of the fiord. He tried unsuccessfully to shut his mind to everything except getting back to the beach.

He paddled steadily onwards. Behind him the camp was still a battleground between fire and flood. Another small fire had broken out in spite of the spreading waters; another small light to mark his journey, to remind him of their successful attack. Yet he was hardly aware of the fight between fire and water. His mind was filled with the clamour of a different conflict: the conflict between honesty and self-justification. Every blow and counter-blow in that fight struck at his reason.

The arguments swayed back and forth with every stroke of the paddle; the preservation of his sanity depended on reaching the beach as quickly as possible.

When he eventually sighted land it was the wrong place. Large, jagged rocks rose menacingly before him, rocks which would slice into his rubber boat as soon as he ran it on to them. He recollected how they had just missed their proper landfall at the edge of the camp and had let the dinghy drift a little distance along the shore. He dug his paddle deep into the water, swung the dinghy broadside to the rocks and then one hard pull with the paddle was sufficient to bring him within sight of their beach. At that opportune moment there was yet another small explosion in the camp, a new fire broke out and illuminated the last few yards of his journey. With a last savage stroke he drove the dinghy up on to the beach they had left a lifetime ago.

He climbed slowly from the dinghy, his stiffened legs throbbed painfully. He ripped off his gloves, hurriedly massaged his thighs, then turned to help Reilly. He threw aside Reilly's gun and tried to drag him out of the dinghy. The slack weight of the body and the flabby, yielding sides of the boat completely defeated him.

He tried to revive Reilly as he lay in the dinghy; if he regained consciousness he might help himself a little. But he did not revive. Harding put his hand on Reilly's face; it was icy — but that was understandable — he was bound to be cold and wet. He could not detect any evidence he was breathing, but Reilly was relaxed and breathing very gently. He tried to get his arms under Reilly's shoulders so he could lift him, but he was too heavy and Harding was too exhausted. He pulled his hands out from under Reilly's back and felt the stickiness on his fingers. Before the protecting, rationalising part of his self could remind him of the mud they had crawled through the truth had pierced his brain.

Some time later he came to his senses lying on the beach, childishly sobbing into his sleeve. His right shoulder, the one he had strained coming down the mountainside, felt as if it was on fire. The strain of lifting Reilly had made it worse. Lifting Reilly!

He staggered to his feet, confused memories stirring his dulled mind. He had some vague recollection of having kicked out at the dinghy; kicking the body, cursing it in a high screaming voice he had not recognised as his own. Had he given away his position? How long had he been on the beach? He peered into the smashed face of his watch. He did not remember breaking it.

He tottered to the water's edge and looked down into the dinghy now rocking gently half in and half out of the water, cradling its pathetic burden between its stout, pneumatic flanks. He looked at the body for some time, still unbelieving, still hoping that Reilly would suddenly stir; that this bright, hard, dynamic man would rise up, take command and help him.

The slow realisation that this would never happen revived the creeping cancer of fear within him; the need to save his own neck began to gnaw at his mind. He had to get away. He looked across the black water. Fires still burned; the steady, pounding of water falling from the dam still came dully across the rippled surface of the fiord. He had to get away; get away before the Germans recovered sufficiently to start searching for their attackers. He had to get back to the cave in time to send the key message. He had to go and he had to cover his retreat as well as he could. But how? What would Reilly do? What would Reilly do if he were alive and it was he, Harding, who was dead? Then he knew.

He drew his knife, pricked a hole in the side of the dinghy and stood listening to the hiss of escaping gas. Then he pushed the dinghy out into the water, pushed it out until he was almost waist deep. Oblivious of the freezing cold, he stood in the water and watched the dinghy drift slowly away from him, slowly disappearing into the flame-flecked night. Then he walked backwards out of the water, never taking his eyes off the dark place where Reilly had been borne away like some proud Viking.

On the beach he found Reilly's

Schmiesser. He picked it up, swung it round over his head and flung it far out into the water. As the plume of spray momentarily hung in the air it was matched by a tongue of flame which leapt through the roof of one of the camp buildings. In that red light he saw the dinghy for the last time, moving slowly but steadily into the deep, quiet waters.

He felt a strange light-headedness sweep over him. It was nearly over and then he would be free. He was free to climb back to the cave, send a message, free to escape. He was in sight of the end of racking fears, of being burdened with terrors. His empty hands, his lack of weapons symbolised his emancipation. He would climb the mountain side before him in record time, unencumbered, unworried. At that moment the dreadful, horrible truth seared him. His hands should not be empty. The papers: he had nearly gone without them. Where was the black bag that contained the summary notes of their research? Those precious files were justification of his own survival. He began to run along the water's edge looking for the bag. Then he stopped. He knew where it was. It was under Reilly's legs.

It was still in the dinghy. All that effort, weeks of effort, all the killing, and now the bag, the great prize, was in the drifting dinghy, far, far beyond his reach.

He smashed his fists into his face and stood locked in a terrible rigidity of despair. It was for this that Rogstad had been murdered. It was for this that Jones had struggled on, his hand pressed to his side, holding his life together for as long as possible. For this had Reilly died, probably Hurst and Cooper also. Slowly, he wiped the blood from his mouth and, as he did so, his mind was mercifully wiped clear of all anguish, all agony of self-reproach. The unthinkable and unspeakable might not have happened.

He walked briskly across the beach until he found the deep rut which Reilly had carved in the sand. At the base of the tree to which it pointed he found the two water bottles and Reilly's pack. He put one bottle in the pack and swung it on to his back; the other bottle and the pump he threw into the fiord. Then he untied the rope from the tree and began to haul himself up the slope. Every step was automatic; no thought, no feeling troubled him as he climbed, reeling in the rope as he went. When he reached the upper end of the rope he untied it and put the coil into the rucksack.

The next section of the climb was not roped. He had to find his way through the blackness relying on his compass and on the fluorescent paint marks on the tree trunks. These marks were all on the upslope side of the trees so that he had to look backwards and downwards to find them. The result was inevitable: when he had covered about fifty yards he turned to look down the slope and blundered into a tree. He was not moving very quickly but in his exhausted condition the collision was violent enough to bring him to his knees. He put his hand to his left cheek which he had scraped against the tree trunk and rubbed it gently. Then he fell on to his side and rolled down the slope until he struck another tree.

He rose to his feet a different person.

Gone was the grey, protective mist in his mind; gone the false composure under which he had been sheltering. The bitter realities of what he had done and had still to do were seeping back into his consciousness. The awareness of these things sharpened more quickly and cut more deeply than his growing awareness of his physical suffering. His thoughts and actions became strangely interrelated, almost entangled with each other.

Can't be much further to the next roped section. I'll be glad to get to a steeper section with fewer pine needles. Climbing over ground covered with them is like wallowing in treacle. Reilly said that when he came back from seeing Hurst away in his dinghy. Is Hurst in his dinghy now? Will he meet Reilly on his way? God! God! What can I say if he finds that bag and brings it back with him? Wait. Look, Major, the radio messages are the most important part of my job. I had to travel light to get back to the radio in time. After all, I did take a risk returning unarmed. There's a paint mark. I'm on course. Going in the right direction. Are

Hurst and Cooper going in the right directions? If Hurst is not on his way back by boat he won't bump into the dinghy. The bag was very heavy. Had more than a dozen files in it. I had only to look at the top one to see what Carl was up to. Poor old Carl. What brought him to this terrible place? Strange the coincidence that Reilly shot him before I got into the office. What would I have done if I had recognised him before he was shot? He would not have known me under my beard and blacking. I could not have shot him. But I could not have shot anyone with that safety catch. Dear God, what a fool! What's that rope for? Made it. Rope's nice. Good rope. Deserve a rest.

Now get on. Strange how low branches hit me in the face. Didn't happen on the way down. Dared not because Joe was with me. God it hurts. My shoulder hurts. It's slowing me more than the pain in my legs. Breathing getting painful too. But I'm warmer, drying out. Funny not remembering getting soaked to the waist. Must have been all that water we got in the dinghy. Careful! That's taken the skin right off the shin bone. God, it hurts! Rocks very slippery here. Probably my boots, they're still pretty full. Water's oozing out and making soles slippery. Get moving. Keep going. Must press on. Dawn soon. Still very dark in the trees but not for long. Should have taken Joe's watch as mine is broken. Can't remember if I spotted it was broken before or after the dinghy drifted away. I never thought. Never do, do you? Never thought. I didn't mean it. I forgot all about the notes because of Joe. Please don't let them find out. Please God, please, please, please . . . End of rope. Untie put in pack. Put.

Get up! Get up! Germans might be coming. Can't climb up if I take away ropes. Stop Germans climbing so fast. Hurst would say 'stop Jerry'. All one of them? One, one. Check compass yourself you are the only one here. A paint mark. Joe's mark. Yes, Joe, on course. You know all about it, Joe. You wouldn't let them find out. You know what it did to us. All that noise, fires, fire bombs, screaming, shooting, waiting. Waiting was the worst, even worse than you shooting those men in the office. All I thought was widows and orphans and widows . . .

All dead, everyone dead. Everywhere. Only me. No need to say. Say nothing. We saw enough to answer all questions without their notes. Best to forget. Need not say a word.

Must rest. Sit here. Drink. Steady on! Need water for morning. In the morning. Morning can't be far away. No mist so bomb-aimers can see. Not that that matters much. Joe and I did not leave much that matters. Did not leave. It's no good, sonny, as Joe would say. No good, sonny. You know. *You always will know*. You can't pretend to yourself. You forgot them. You forgot them. Forgot, forgot, forgotforgotforgot. Stop! Take it easy. Easy. Still two things to do. There's that last stretch to climb where you fell on Reilly coming down. You've got to climb that. You've got to work the radio. Take it easy.

Tears. Feeble tears. You wouldn't dare if Reilly, if Joe. Gently, gently. Nearly there, so easy. Take it easy. Here's the tree. Undo rope. Pack's full of rope, so put this one on outside. Nearly there. Last bit, nearly up. Nothing to worry. Last bit. Nearly. No worries now. No worries. No.

19

The awakening was like an earlier awakening. He lay face down on the bed, his clenched fists pulling at the under-sheet. A voice in his head was shouting: 'No! No! Don't say it! Don't tell me! Let me sleep!' He had longed for sleep to bear him away, to be a refuge from his father's voice, a voice too eager to tell him the news. 'I'm very sorry, son. Mother had decided. There's nothing I can do.' The voice was flooded with self-pity. 'She will not enter this house again.' Momentarily the voice sounded harder, but he was not deceived. He knew it was his mother's choice and not his father's determination which had caused the smash. Mother's choice. And what would they say at school? He burrowed under the clothes, stopped up his ears. His father muttered some feeble protest and then left the room. He did not call him back; he feared his father because he dreaded the possibility he might grow up to be like him. The bed smelt vilely of sweat and damp; the mattress was very hard. He pushed his head out into the open. He was in his sleeping bag in the cave. Twenty years peeled away in an instant leaving him exposed to the present.

He was alone. Neither Cooper nor Hurst had shaken him awake. An alarm clock within him had dragged him back to consciousness. He stood up and rubbed his eyes. He fumbled for the torch and began to look for the watch Reilly had left on top of the radio. He stared at the watch face. The time was now. Now! He had to send now if the aircraft were to be diverted from their alternative target. By some miracle he had woken up just in time. Now! Just a quick check outside first and he would be ready. He staggered to the mouth of the cave and looked out.

The sky was lighter in the east but he could see nothing in the valley. All the fires were out. How long had he slept? Why had he got into the sleeping bag? Had someone helped him? He rushed through the caves flashing his torch to see if someone was there, lying wounded or unconscious in a dark corner. He found no one. While he was searching he tried to remember the details of his arrival at the cave but his mind could only carry him to the moment when he untied the last length of rope. He remembered nothing after that.

All too readily his mind began to drag him back to what had happened at the bottom of the valleyside, on the beach, in the dinghy, in the camp. He pushed it all aside. For the last time in his life he fought to take full control of his mind; to carry out the very last of his duties. The action of switching on the transmitter helped to clear his head of everything except the essential operational information now required of him. The same action switched off the mass of pain his body was feeling; his mind refused to accept the messages passed to it by his tortured flesh.

The radio was alive, little lights glowing. The faintest crackling through the headphones, and then clear; so clear he doubted anyone was listening. His cracked lips rasped under his tongue. He glanced at the watch. He was a minute late.

'Clover here. Clover here. Are you receiving me? Are you receiving me? Over.'

'Reaper here. Reaper here. We hear you. We hear you. Hold. Hold.' Harding waited. What a bizarre choice of code names. What a choice. The black, blank wall in his mind shut off his thoughts. He waited, unthinking, unmoving; merely a valve in the set, alive within himself, but fixed, screwed tight.

'Hello Clover. Hello Clover. All systems receive you. All systems receive you. Do you understand? Over.'

'Yes, Reaper. I understand.' All systems included the crews of the aircraft, who would now listen to every word, including some coded information which they would not understand.

'Diamonds are soft. Diamonds are soft. Do you hear me Reaper? Over.' They had to hear that message; it told them the enemy was working in the same field of research as the British and Americans, but that they were a long way behind.

'Reaper hears you. Diamonds are soft. Diamonds are soft.' It was at that moment Harding knew he was talking to the Brigadier and knew what the next question would be.

'Reaper asks how many leaves are on the clover? How many leaves? Over.' Harding stayed in control, even as the first tears ran down his face. The others might turn up but he didn't believe it. In any case he had to answer on the basis of the situation at that moment.

'There is one leaf on the clover. There is one leaf on the clover. This is the second leaf. This is the second leaf. Over.'

'Message understood. Are you all right? Over.'

'Yes. Yes. Over.'

'We hear you Clover. We hear you very well. I suggest there is no need for repetition with such good reception. Check reception with Apple. Over.'

'Understood, Reaper. You listen in. You listen in.'

'Clover calling A for Apple. Clover

calling A for Apple. Are you receiving me? Over.'

'Apple hears Clover. We hear you loud and clear so don't bother repeating to us either. How are things there, old boy?' Harding did not reply at once but sat before the set marvelling at the clarity of the reception, and at the extraordinary casualness of the Squadron Leader's voice. It occurred to him that he must sound extremely jumpy and tensed up. Perhaps the man was trying to help him remain calm.

'Things are good for you, Apple. Easterly wind, high cloud, ground expected to be clear. I will confirm later. Over.'

'A for Apple here. Good show. All the dancers can hear the music. Stand by for sonata. Over.'

'I hear sonata. I hear sonata. Out.' All was well. All the radio operators could hear him. Sonata was the code word telling him E.T.A. was half an hour away. No further messages would be transmitted until the aircraft were near the target; there was no point in helping the Germans work out exactly what was going on. He switched off the radio. He had completed the first stage of the job and somewhere, perhaps in Bergen, the unsuspecting civilians could go on sleeping. No bombs would fall on them today.

He had half an hour to clear up the cave and prepare for his departure; half an hour to keep his mind occupied with trivialities. He had to forget the great bloated maggot of fear, feeding on his living entrails, swelling up with his own blood and choking him. He removed his headphones and looked towards the cave entrance. The first thing he saw was Reilly's rucksack full of ropes; ropes which the Sergeant had set up to help him. It was unbearable. Reilly's kit to be handled. He remembered Joe's lecture yesterday, only yesterday, Joe trying to tell him not to step out of line. He had accepted his position of inferiority almost willingly. For Joe Reilly he had felt a kind of affection. He could not face the prospect of sorting his kit; not now. He was supposed to do it now as preparation for his escape but the task was beyond him. He had to get out, get away from the bereft heaps of their possessions; he had to get out of the cave.

He crept on to the ledge, taking with him his sleeping-bag, camera, binoculars, watch, headphones and microphone. The leads to the transmitter snaked out of the cave after him across the cold stone. He spread out his sleeping bag and arranged his equipment round it. As he did so he kept his eyes averted from the view below him. There would be time enough for that.

There was no sign of a dinghy on the water. His shaking hands directed the glasses towards the camp. He did not recognise it at first and fiddled with the focus of the binoculars. Then he realised what had happened: the camp was completely changed. It hardly seemed necessary to call in the R.A.F. It would be a wasted journey for them. But perhaps not. He had only entered one building; other buildings might be almost as important. More than half the structures were quite undamaged; those that were well away from the area of the rock fall and those that had not caught fire. The important thing now was that the bomb aimers must be told what to expect. This information had to be given them at the very last moment in case the description of the damage was picked up by the Germans and they recognised the target. Even more likely was the possibility that the enemy would get a fix on his position while he was transmitting. Of course, the bombers would be detected on radar but there was no need to pinpoint the target for the Luftwaffe. His job was to pinpoint it for his own side.

He wondered what the target would look like from twelve thousand feet. There would be just enough light for the pilots to pick their way along the coast, swing inland and come driving along the line of the fiord. At the east end all they would see was the great patch of shadow, until someone dropped the brilliant red and green markers straight into the pit. Even if they missed the camp they would be clear enough for Harding to refer to as indicators. It must be strange to bomb a target which cannot be seen; worse still, a target which might show little reaction to exploding bombs. Of course, there would be fires but nothing very spectacular; less spectacular than a smouldering cigarette end in all that dulling shadow. They might not even see that much if the rising sun dazzled them. Odd to think that the aircrews would see the sun before he did. He looked at his watch: time to hear from them. He crawled into the cave and switched on the set.

'A for Apple calling Clover. A for Apple calling Clover. Are you receiving me? Are you receiving me? Over.'

'Clover here. I am receiving you loud and clear I suggest you transmit without repetition. No repetition. Over.'

'Good show. It's the same for us. Now, if you're ready on your ringside seat we will start the show. So stand by, Clover. Stand by. Over.'

'Standing by, A for Apple. The next move is yours. Over.'

'A for Apple calling all aircraft. Come in, please. Come in. Over.'

Harding listened as the leader checked his team. There was no reply from C for

329

Charlie and O for Oscar. Harding wondered why but wasted no time interrupting. When the leader had checked his team he called Harding again.

'Clover here,' replied Harding. 'Here is the information on the target for your markers. Are you ready? Over.'

'A for Apple here, boy. Our marker aircraft is N for Nutmeg. We can all hear you but thought introductions were in order; especially as N for Nutmeg is a Wellington. Carry on, N for Nutmeg. Over.'

'N for Nutmeg here, sport. Tell us about the target. Even if we can't see the bugger we like to know what's what. Over.' The warm, rough Australian accent somehow reminded Harding of Reilly. He felt the tenuous link slip back in his mind. No time now.

'Hello, N for Nutmeg. Clover here. The target has been mauled a bit. The dam is broken and the water is still trickling over the edge of it. Much of the camp is flooded so you may have trouble picking out the coast line.' Someone swore softly across the air.

'Sorry, Clover. It's just that the coast is one of the few lines we thought we might pick out. Carry on.'

'On the south side of the camp the whole mountain-side has fallen down. The buildings labelled M, N, O, P, and S have disappeared, as has part of the sports field. The fallen rocks extend far enough south-west to wipe out the line of the beach at that point. Sorry about that, Nutmeg. The other change that stands out from where I am is that buildings J and E on your plan are completely burnt out. That completes the list of main changes. Over.'

'Jesus, boy! You fellers must have had a bloody good party. Thanks for the tips, anyhow. We're coming in now. Stand by all crew members and keep your eyes skinned. Stand by bomb aimer.'

'I'm ready, Skipper. Let's go.'

In the silence that followed, Harding kept his glasses on the camp. Then he heard the sound of engines; but it was not the sound he expected, nor was it from the right direction. The noise came from below him. He saw the motor launch pulling away from the dormitory block and turning towards the camp. The boat appeared to be full. Just in time to be blown to pieces, thought Harding. I suppose that boat has been ferrying back and forth all night but I didn't hear it.

A new sound began to echo in the great valley. The steady roar of aircraft engines became louder and increasingly distorted as the noise slammed backward and forward between the mountain slopes. The Wellington shot into view over the shoulder of the plateau on his right. It was flying much lower and faster than he had anticipated. The reason for using a Wellington instead of one of the four-engined bombers was immediately obvious as the pilot pulled on the control column and easily lifted the aircraft over the top of the shattered dam. Harding was not to know he was watching a relatively new idea in target marking. Before he could ask any questions the radio was buzzing with comments.

'Markers not released that time, Skipper. Couldn't see a bloody thing. You'll have to go round again.' A furious discussion broke out about the best way to tackle the problem, but Harding missed much of what was said, partly because reception deteriorated as the aircraft swung behind high ground to the east, partly because he was bewildered by the noise of the engines and the incredible speed at which everything had happened. He would have sworn the plane had actually flown past him *below* the Lion Head, even though common sense told him otherwise. From the row going on he gathered this was partly the trouble. The bomb aimer kept explaining that he was so near the ground, and the plane was moving so fast, he could not hope to mark the target, especially as all he could see was shadows and water. He urged the pilot either to dive-bomb the target or, if they had to be straight and level, come in slower and higher.

While this was being discussed, Harding saw the main bomber force for the first time. The aircraft were riding very high, apparently motionless far to the west. He only spotted them because the sun was glinting on their wings. They appeared infinitely remote, infinitely beautiful; as remote from him as were the events of yesterday. Today was to be so different. The pulsing roar of the Wellington's engines jerked him back to reality.

The second attempt was tragically different from the first. The bomber came in, straight and level at about five thousand feet; her engines throttled back so she moved at little more than stalling speed. This time the Germans were ready for her. They could only muster a pair of machine-guns but that was sufficient. They opened fire as soon as the Wellington was within range.

The pilot held the plane rock steady while the bomb aimer released the markers. Harding could see the bullets tearing strips out of the fuselage, knew they must be hitting vital centres in the plane because the radio was silent and none of the gunners returned the fire. The fuselage began to glow red, the engines roared uselessly as the nose dropped. Harding could see the aircraft swelling with fire as it drove past him. The pilot could not lift the nose, so tried to turn the aircraft away from the hills and into the north-pointing toe of the valley. He must have known it was useless, knowing the fiord ended at the foot of a towering mountain wall. Perhaps he hoped to get down in the water. The stricken aircraft vanished from sight round the shoulder of the highland.

Harding heard the flat thump of the explosion without seeing the final disastrous ending; he never knew if the aircraft had exploded in the air or had plunged into the mountain. All he saw was the wind-ruffled surface of the fiord suddenly heaving into wild motion, as a chaotic pattern of waves began to cut across the surface from the hidden northern end.

Harding retched painfully. As he wiped his mouth with the back of his hand he suddenly realised why there had been no reply from C for Charlie and O for Oscar. They had also crashed. They must have been caught by German night-fighters returning to base. Only the low fuel levels in the fighters' tanks had saved the bombers from a worse mauling. He could not understand how he knew this to be true. Only one other fact mattered: the markers were down. He called up the commander.

'Calling A for Apple. Bad news I'm afraid — '

'Save your breath, Clover. We saw it from here. Did the markers land in the right place? Over.'

'Oh. Eh — yes. Yes, A for Apple.' (Was everyone but himself completely single-minded?) 'The red markers are central. The green markers are about two hundred yards to the west; they are nearly all floating on the water. Over.'

'Everyone heard that, did they?' Each crew repeated the message, identifying themselves as they did so. No one paused to hear from C for Charlie and O for Oscar.

'Right! We attack exactly as planned and with no delays. There is low cloud moving in fast from the east. Attack!'

Harding looked up. Only one aircraft could be seen. It was coming closer, straight and level at twelve thousand feet. Harding looked down into the camp and, even at that distance, got the impression of frantic activity. The Germans were trying to extinguish the markers and, as Harding watched, two of the red flares were snuffed out. Was it possible that they could put them all out before the first bomb load was released? The Germans obviously thought not; the machine-guns were hammering wildly even though the aircraft was out of range. Harding glared at the aircraft, willing the bombs to fall away. Then he saw them falling.

He ignored the voices chattering through his headphones and watched the bombs as they fell: large plump cases of high explosive, small clusters of incendiaries. They spread out below the belly of the aircraft, fell faster and faster until speed and distance removed them from Harding's sight. He looked down instead. Whether it was imagination or the advantage of a ringside seat he could not tell, but he was sure he saw the bombs again just before they sliced into the mud of the delta.

The explosions ran like a linked chain through the camp and into the cliff below the wrecked dam. The great plumes of mud and smoke rose up like majestic trees, stood for a moment, then collapsed, and in collapsing, revealed their deep, blood-red roots of fire.

In that echo chamber of a valley the noise was both multiplied and distorted. Harding felt as if he was lifted clear of the ledge and flung flat against the rock buttress of the cave entrance. His threshing body knocked the camera off the ledge and down into the forest below. It was only when his scrabbling hands caught at the edge of the sleeping bag that he realised his body had not been moved. The physical experience of so much noise was appalling.

'Come in, Clover. Where are you for Christ's sake? Clover, come in.'

'Sorry, A for Apple. You deafened me a bit. You were right on target. The camp is a shambles. I doubt if there will be any more flak. Bomb on the two fires. Bomb on the two fires.'

The first bombs of the second load fell slightly short and great plumes of water rose white and slender from the fiord. The green markers on the surface rocked wildly as the explosions chopped the water. But other bombs did hit the target and another fire broke out. The red markers had all been replaced by fires. He could hear the crackling explosions of ammunition as the arms store blazed furiously. The machine-guns were silent.

As A for Apple circled overhead the other bombers trundled up to the target and released their mixed loads of incendiary and high explosive death on to the camp. After the sixth bomb load had gone into the maelstrom, A for Apple complained that the target was now obscured by smoke, and asked if there were any parts of the camp they had neglected. Harding reminded them of the dormitory block but doubted if it merited a full bomb load. A for Apple brushed this doubt aside and the next aircraft came in very low, dropped its bombs right on the block and flattened it completely. The motor launch, which had been returning to the block, swung round and stuttered back towards the camp. It disappeared behind the clouds of smoke and Harding never saw it again.

The last bombers came in, the last bombs whistled down, the last hammer blows drove German dreams deep into the black, sour mud of the delta.

'Target destroyed completely,' said Harding.

'We couldn't have done it without you, Clover. Good show.'

'Thank you A for Apple. Good luck to your team now. Over.'

'Thanks, boy. Good luck to you. We're on our way. Over and out.' Harding raised his hands to his headphones but another voice cut in.

'Hello, Clover. Hello, Clover. Reaper here. Reaper here. Are you receiving me? Are you receiving me? Over.'

'Hello, Reaper. The job is done. The job is done. Do you hear that?'

'Steady on, Clover. Yes, I hear you. The job is done. Are you reporting details of diamonds now? Over.'

'No. Over.'

'Very good, Clover. Don't worry about it. Are you clear? Are you clear? Over.'

'How the hell do I know, you fool? Over.'

'Steady on, Clover. Calm down. Are you receiving me? Are you receiving me? Over.'

'Yes. I expect the enemy is as well. Over.' How could he hope to know if he was clear. The Germans might be coming for him already. On the other hand they might be too busy to bother just yet. The camp was an inferno.

'Which letter do you want, Clover? Which letter? Over.' The Brigadier wanted to know the pick-up point. He wanted to know where to send the boat, the — No! No, he could not face that journey again.

'I will not say. I will not say, unless you promise different travel to the first journey. Over.'

'Clover, Clover. What are you talking about? What's the matter? Come in, come in. Over.' Harding did not reply immediately. He sat on the ground and relaxed; enjoying the panic in the Brigadier's voice. He was the man who had sent them to Norway. He was shrieking something at him but Harding was not listening. At last he spoke into the microphone.

'Shut up! Shut up, Reaper! You know exactly what I mean. Do you want me to spell it out over the air? And don't forget I don't have to come back. You know that, don't you?'

'All right, Clover. All right. Please don't worry. We'll look after you. Don't worry, just take things calmly. Over.'

'I am sure you will. You have to, especially as I am the only one left. It is Point Rosemary. Point Rosemary. Over.'

'Thank you, Clover. Point Rosemary understood. Over.'

'Good. Over and Out.' He ripped off the headphones and hurled them back into the cave. The spluttering of the Brigadier's voice was suddenly silenced.

20

He had done what had to be done. As he piled together the sad refuse of the operation his bruised mind led him back along the blood-soaked chain of memory for the last time. Each item he touched raised a ghost within the dark cave, and each ghost led him further from reality and deeper into grief. His exhausted mind, locked within his pain-racked body, was like a fatigued elastic band which had been too often stretched and relaxed. For weeks he had been wrenched back and forth between optimism and doubt, confidence and uncertainty, resignation and biting fear; the last days had accelerated these switches of mood and emotion. The sorting of his colleagues' kit led to the final tightening of his mind before it snapped under the strain.

He did not know, would never know, that this breakdown was to save him from any more war, from any inquisition by the two grey men, and from ever knowing the tragic fate of two grey, ash-grey cities in the Far East. He knew only that he was surrounded by the most terrible silence, but without knowing it was the silence of approaching madness.

Reilly's pack. 'What will you do after the war, Joe?'

'After the war? Why, sonny, there's no after the war for the likes of us. We must be made expendable. Every time we get away with a crazy show like this there's another one laid on. They won't know what to do with us after the war. Your sort will still be useful, but they want the rest of us used up by the time the war ends.'

All used up. All used up.

In Reilly's pack he found the rubber casing for the dinghy. How they had all struggled to pack that thing when training ended. Their failure had infuriated Hurst who was barely civil to the expert called in from the parachute section on the nearby aerodrome. Hurst had built up a team which was supposed to do everything and do everything superbly.

Hurst: the man who saw everything, planned for everything. The face behind the curtain, the watcher; those bulging, steely eyes assessing, always assessing. Yet finally, he had not seen, not seen certain things that really mattered. Eyes like any other eyes being clouded by disbelief, by hope, by too great a concern for his fellows. The vacuum flask belonged to a man who planned for every contingency. Where was he now? Was he under that great pile of boulders, or on his way to the beach? If the fallen mountain was his monument he would be amused that no one would ever know for certain if this was so. Where was he? Had he and Andy escaped?

Then Andy's flask was in his hands. He heard again the shots from the top of the dam. But now he heard something else as well: the sound of an object falling down the dam face as the shots were fired and before the explosion. Had he heard that the first time, or was he now imagining it? Was it Andy falling? If he had fallen he was now in the camp with Carl. All trace lost after the pulverising air raid. That meant posted missing. Carl and Cooper. No record of their death except what he could report. And he could only tell of Carl. The only record was his word. How ironic that was. No files, no photos, no record but his word.

Lavatory paper. He heard his own laughter. That packet of paper epitomised the whole job. Hurst, from his experience wanting to bring it. Jones had laughed. Hurst explained effect on morale and on physical comfort and discomfort when walking far and fast. Jones made some coarse sneering remark. And sneered again when Hurst put it into Harding's pack. 'The right bloke to carry it,' said Jones. Now he could remember nothing else of Jones.

When all the equipment was piled up against the radio he set the charge. His last sane act: to give himself two hours to get clear of the cave. He could hear Hurst's voice giving those instructions even while he did the job. He left the cave and climbed to the plateau. He took no pack and no weapons. He had no further use for them.

He stood above the valley, the grey plateau before him, grey clouds thickening above, grey smoke drifting up from the camp behind him.

He looked down at himself; saw the caked mud, the ripped material which had caught on the cut wire; saw the whitening crust on his drying boots and trousers. His empty, empty hands, cut, bruised, still smeared with blacking. He supposed his face was the same. He put his left hand to his right shoulder; the pain was nagging him again. He felt the hand shaking on the shoulder. Shaking hands. He looked at himself again, knew himself at last. He was Anders Rogstad. He had become that man: Anders Rogstad. He was now the survivor, the successor, the inheritor of all the horror of this war. It was he who was now to wander alone in this harsh, black, northern land. The shaking was suddenly much worse. He was laughing. They had come to the wrong place, anyway. This was not the main German centre. The only conclusion was a negative one. All wasted; all the effort, the courage, the fear, the viciousness, the expertise, the lives all wasted.

He began to walk slowly towards the north-west, across gently undulating ground to the cairn about a mile away. He had to walk for an hour to reach it. When he arrived he sat on the ground with his back against the great mound of rocks. He did not know he had taken an hour to arrive; he only knew he had to rest.

No urgency, no hurry. Had he not survived the German occupation for so long without hurrying or rushing? His friend had not been so fortunate. Was his name Sven? A harmless fellow trying to help out, but he had had no training, no training. What had happened to him?

He rested, not hearing the soughing wind nor the fine needles of rain rattling on to his anorak hood. He leaned back against the cairn and raised his head. The sound of his laughter rose into the grey clouds and was lost.

We do hope that you have enjoyed reading this large print book.

Did you know that all of our titles are available for purchase?

We publish a wide range of high quality large print books including:
Romances, Mysteries, Classics
General Fiction
Non Fiction and Westerns

Special interest titles available in large print are:
The Little Oxford Dictionary
Music Book, Song Book
Hymn Book, Service Book

Also available from us courtesy of Oxford University Press:
Young Readers' Dictionary
(large print edition)
Young Readers' Thesaurus
(large print edition)

For further information or a free brochure, please contact us at:
Ulverscroft Large Print Books Ltd.,
The Green, Bradgate Road, Anstey,
Leicester, LE7 7FU, England.
Tel: (00 44) **0116 236 4325**
Fax: (00 44) **0116 234 0205**

Other titles in the
Linford Mystery Library:

ACCOUNT SETTLED

John Russell Fearn

When scientist Rajek Quinton was pushed, screaming, down a mineshaft by Emerson Drew's hired killer, Drew and his co-conspirators Darnhome and de Brock were set to exploit Quinton's amazing invention. But he reckoned without Larry Clark of the C.I.D., and Quinton's genius. Larry, aided by Drew's secretary, Joyce Sutton, obtained the evidence needed to send Drew and his cohorts to their doom. But exactly who was Joyce Sutton? And did Quinton really die in the mud-filled pit shaft?